"Good afternoon, I'm Olivia Wyatt. Welcome to Table of Hope."

The man turned his face toward hers. As their eyes met, she felt a powerful spark shoot through her system.

"Heath Stone." He stood and reached to shake her hand. "Detective Biddle said you'd be expecting me."

Olivia took a second to compare the reality before her with the computer hacker she'd agreed to take in while he worked off a hundred hours of community service.

If this guy's an internet nerd, I'm a Mexican drug lord.

Olivia had been warned that beneath Heath Stone's quiet exterior there was a clever cybercriminal. Well, growing up around a lying father and then earning a degree in social work had taught Olivia a thing or two about men. Not only would she keep a close eye on Mr. Stone, she'd keep him busy with laundry, cooking, cleaning and Bible study.

But how would she keep herself from staring at those *dangerous* eyes?

Books by Mae Nunn

Love Inspired

Hearts in Bloom
*Sealed with a Kiss
*Amazing Love
*Mom in the Middle
*Lone Star Courtship
A Texas Ranger's Family
Her Forever Family
A Season for Family

*Texas Treasures

MAE NUNN

grew up in Houston and graduated from the University of Texas with a degree in communications. When she fell for a transplanted Englishman living in Atlanta, she moved to Georgia and made an effort to behave like a Southern belle. But when she found that her husband was quite agreeable to life as a born-again Texan, Mae happily returned to her cowgirl roots and cowboy boots! In 2008 Mae retired from thirty years of corporate life to focus on her career as a Christian author. When asked how she felt about writing full-time for Steeple Hill Books, Mae summed up her response with one word: "Yeeeee-haw!"

A Season for Family
Mae Nunn

Steeple
Hill®

Published by Steeple Hill Books™

STEEPLE HILL BOOKS

Steeple Hill®

ISBN-13: 978-0-373-81514-2

A SEASON FOR FAMILY

Recycling programs
for this product may
not exist in your area.

www.SteepleHill.com

Printed in U.S.A.

Jesus replied, "Love the Lord your God with all your heart and with all your soul, and with all your mind. This is the first and greatest commandment. And the second is like it: Love your neighbor as yourself. All the law and the prophets hang on these two commandments."

—*Matthew* 22:37–40

A Season for Family is dedicated to
Bill and Peggy Biddle.

Your love for one another, your courage in the face
of adversity and your faith in our Lord Jesus Christ
is an inspiration to everyone who knows and loves
the two of you.

Acknowledgments

With love and thanks to my son, Paul Nunn, just
the skeptical male I needed in my life while I was
developing the character of Heath Stone.

Special thanks and appreciation go to Alan Beck
for sharing your amazing stories and years of
experience as an undercover officer.

Thank you to Pat Magid of Studio Gallery
in Waco, Texas, for answering all my questions,
even the dumb ones.

I'm grateful to My Brother's Keeper in Waco, Texas,
for the tour, the education and the incredible work
you do for the people you serve.

As always, I owe my deepest gratitude to Michael.
I am forever in your debt for being my critique
partner, my first line editor and my biggest fan.
You make it all worthwhile, my darlin'.

Lastly, special thanks to Libo
for keeping me company.

Chapter One

The buzzer installed at Table of Hope's bullet-proof security door echoed through the hallway, signaling to Olivia Wyatt that she had a visitor. Somebody needed to get inside the homeless mission and out of the gusting wind, which was unusually cold for Waco, Texas, even in November. The converted warehouse was perpetually locked from the inside since it was in a dicey, old part of town that was beyond the reach of revitalization.

"I got it, Miss Livvy," Velma called from the check-in desk.

Olivia was elbow-deep in a carton of jeans donated for her shelter's clients when Velma swept into the women's sleeping quarters a few minutes later and swooned across a lower bunk with Scarlett O'Hara flair.

"If you're already worn out, it's gonna be a

long night for me," Olivia said, doubting that fatigue had anything to do with her buddy's the-atrics. Velma was a natural drama queen.

"Not tired, just need some smelling salts after bein' up close to what just came through the front door," she insisted, fanning herself and rolling playful eyes. Though she was prone to exaggeration, this was excessive even for Velma.

"Let me guess—Brad Pitt needs a place to stay tonight?" Olivia continued sorting clothes.

"This man's every bit as good lookin' but more in a Johnny Depp with a shaved head kinda way. And he's asking for you, so go take a look at those dangerous eyes for yourself." Velma sat up, crossed stubby legs campfire-style and reached for a plus-size pair of secondhand denims.

Olivia turned her full attention to the conversation.

"Really, he asked for me?"

"Said his name's Stone but looks more like velvet," Velma giggled and fake shuddered.

Olivia couldn't help laughing at her friend, a key member of the core group accepted for Table of Hope's resident program. Working side-by-side with her small team was changing Olivia's life as much as it was changing theirs.

By the grace of God her dream of providing homeless outreach had become a reality when they'd served their first meal on a sultry summer evening five months earlier. The days had scattered like fall leaves and now a Thanksgiving wreath made of yellow and orange gourds decorated the front door. It was a perfect complement to the building she'd painted rooster red with green shutters to make it inviting in spite of the burglar bars on every window.

"If I'm lyin' I'm dyin', Miss Livvy," Velma insisted. "He's all wrapped up in a black jacket with a hood probably to hide jailhouse tattoos. But this one smells real nice."

"Girl." Olivia slurred the word as Velma would. "You need to get a grip and stop carrying on every time a clean man walks through our door."

Velma pointed toward the hallway. "Take a gander at that tall drink o' water for yourself." She fanned both hands before her chubby face.

"Okay," Olivia gave in. "I wasn't expecting Mr. Stone until tomorrow but now's as good a time as any to get started. I need to stretch the kinks out of my legs and check on dinner anyway."

She pushed to her feet and enjoyed the pleasant cracking of her spine as she arched her back. Twenty strides carried her out of the women's sleeping quarters, down the corridor past the laundry area and around the corner to the front lobby. Just as Velma had said, a long slender male body was folded into one of the reception chairs, his shrouded head and a pencil poised over a clipboard questionnaire.

"Good afternoon, I'm Olivia Wyatt." She extended her hand.

The man straightened in the chair, turning his face toward hers. As their eyes met, she wanted to wince from the powerful connection that sent a spark sizzling through her central nervous system. Velma's description of his *dangerous eyes* was right on the money.

"Heath Stone." He stood and reached to exchange the courtesy. "Detective Biddle said you'd be expecting me."

Olivia took a split second to compare the reality before her with the computer hacker she'd agreed to take in while he worked off a hundred hours of community service.

If this guy's an Internet nerd, I'm a Mexican drug lord.

From the way Heath Stone had been described to her, Olivia expected a geek, complete with pocket protector. Detective Biddle had called earlier in the day to ask a big favor. Since the Waco computer crimes detective had become something of a benefactor to Table of Hope, Olivia was more than willing to repay his kindness. She agreed to accept Stone into her program while he worked off his sentence for hacking into the city's Intranet.

She'd been warned that beneath Stone's quiet and somewhat sulking exterior there was a skilled and clever cyber criminal. Well, growing up around a lying father and then earning a degree in social work had taught Olivia a thing or two about recognizing the lies of men. She'd not only keep a close eye on Mr. Stone, she'd keep him busy with laundry, cooking, cleaning and Bible study.

She accepted the hand he'd shoved outward, squared her shoulders a bit and returned his stare.

Undercover officer Heath Stone locked eyes with the woman before him as she pressed her warm palm into his cold grip. He felt the pads of Olivia Wyatt's fingers, dry and calloused. If the lady wasn't afraid of physical labor, she just might be bold enough to let her old man run recreational drugs through this innocent-looking place.

"Welcome to Table of Hope," she sounded sincere enough. "I'm glad you made it this evening. We can always use help with dinner service."

The raven-haired beauty he was assigned to check out would put this year's crop of Texas debutantes to shame. Her baggy, pinkish sweater and faded jeans fell across feminine curves on a frame that looked to be about five-foot-ten.

She reminded him of that girl who married Tom Cruise, but with more flesh on her bones.

Heath liked tall women, admired the few who realized stature was an asset. Instead of slouching and rounding her shoulders to camouflage an inch or two, this lady stretched her spine, held her head high, even lifted her chin to stare at him with confident eyes.

Her body language left no doubt that she was in charge.

First impressions count. He hadn't anticipated such a positive one from a woman suspected of having connections to a Mexican drug cartel. But Heath learned early in his career as a cop that looking innocent didn't make a dope dealer any less of a criminal.

"You can fill out that paperwork later." She indicated the clipboard, and then jerked her thumb toward the corridor. "Come with me and we'll put you to work."

Obviously expecting he'd do as she instructed, the lady turned around, headed down the hall at a fast clip and disappeared through an open doorway.

"Oh, and pull the lobby door closed behind you, please!" she hollered.

He slung a backpack over his shoulder and followed orders, looking left and right as he passed down the wide corridor ablaze from the jumble of wild colors on the walls. To his right a large room was filled with several rows of barracks-style bunks covered in bright blue blankets. Most were empty but on a couple of mattresses men curled on their sides, sleeping. On another bunk a guy was stretched out, feet crossed comfortably, a book balanced on his chest.

"Hey, buddy," the reader said, looking up from his book. "Welcome."

Heath lifted a hand, jerked his head and then turned away. He paused beside the next door marked MEN'S LOCKER ROOM, listened until he heard the flush of a toilet.

"You need some personal time?" Olivia Wyatt poked her head back into view.

"No, ma'am. Sorry to drag my feet. I was just lookin' around."

"No apology necessary. I'd normally give you the tour right away but we need to get busy in here." She motioned for him to follow.

"Yes, ma'am." He lengthened his stride to join her in a room that turned out to be the kitchen.

"Please, call me Olivia. *Ma'am* makes me feel ancient and I'm only twenty-seven."

"I hear ya." He shucked off his jacket, hung it on a wall peg atop his backpack. Heath raised his voice to be heard over the rattling of pots nearby. "I know it's a nicety mamas teach their kids in the South, but when anybody calls me *sir*

I can't help lookin' around to see if some feeble old geezer is right behind me."

She handed him a white chef's apron and grabbed one for herself. He followed her lead as she dropped the neck strap over her head and tied the strings behind her back. Then they moved past see-through shelves of canned goods and into a cavernous place painted in fall colors, as if somebody had splattered the walls with pumpkin pie and caramel apples.

The kitchen was rimmed by ovens and cooktops with the middle reserved for butcher block tables. A scrawny gray-haired man and a guy about Heath's age worked over piles of vegetables.

"Amos and Bruce, this is Heath Stone, our new addition to the resident program."

The two might as well have ignored the introduction as they exchanged a glance. The younger one barely nodded, the older one grunted as they continued their duties.

Olivia caught Heath's eye. "They're busy getting the jump on tomorrow's dinner." She stopped next to a row of huge stockpots, lifted a lid and poked a long-handled fork at something inside.

"Thursday's always vegetable soup day," Bruce said matter-of-factly. "Best you ever ate."

The other man grumbled something under his breath and kept his head down, revealing a bald spot. He continued to add to his mound of carrots.

"We always make plenty. Some people come from the other side of town for a bowl of Miss Livvy's soup."

"Bruce, you have three months before you need to start buttering me up for an extension."

The two laughed. Even the old guy managed to contort his face into a grin of sorts.

"Will you wash up and give me a hand with this, please?" Olivia held a couple of quilted mitts toward Heath. "These potatoes are ready to be mashed, but I need you to drain the water off first. Over there." She pointed to one of several deep sinks.

He quickly soaped and rinsed his hands, donned the mitts and then carefully dodged the blistering curtain of steam that rose off the potatoes as they drained into a wire colander. "Thanks for the gloves."

"Good kitchen help is hard to find. We try not to injure a new recruit on his first day." She placed a mixing bowl about half the size of the Astrodome on the counter before him.

"Now what?" Heath waited for instructions.

"We ain't got time to hold your hand," Amos barked.

"Sorry, sir," Heath responded to the jibe. "I'm better with a Mac than macaroni."

"Oh, a wise guy," the older man bristled. "Well, if you're gonna stay with us for a while you'd better get acquainted with the business end of a potato masher."

Olivia handed Heath a utensil with a zigzag shape on one end. He brought it close to his face and studied the strange kitchen tool, trying to recall if he'd ever seen anything like it.

"I was planning to leave you in Bruce and Amos's capable hands, but I've got some time to help out since I'm already prepared for tonight's Bible study."

Bible study?

Before he could question her last comment Olivia got busy giving him a cooking lesson. She scooped a portion of the steaming potatoes into the stainless steel bowl and then squashed away like she was working off a grudge.

"I think my mother used instant potatoes or maybe an electric mixer. Wouldn't that be faster?"

"Look, Steve Jobs," Amos snapped, "money don't grow on trees around here. We make do with what's donated. We only have one big mixer and it's busy smoothin' the lumps out of Bruce's pitiful excuse for gravy." He pointed toward a machine humming away on a countertop across the room.

"So I used a little too much flour," Bruce

defended himself. "Lighten up, *old geezer.*" He emphasized the insult.

Amos snarled and cast a menacing scowl toward Bruce.

"Okay, you two. Give it a rest," Olivia insisted. "Nobody will notice a few lumps in the gravy once it's poured over the potatoes."

Amos turned his glare toward Heath. "We'll never know unless Miss Livvy gets some help."

"Sorry." Heath reached toward Olivia who handed over the masher. He dumped more boiled potatoes into the bowl as she'd done and began to mash with gusto, little gobs flying as he worked. He eventually got a tub of chunky, starchy gunk for his effort.

When he paused, Olivia handed him a spoon and they each took a sample mouthful.

"Kinda boring and gloppy, huh?" he asked, pretty sure nobody would want to eat the stuff.

She nodded, her smile sympathetic as she reached for a cup of water to wash down the bite.

Heath stared down at the mess. "Ugly, too," he admitted.

"I'll take it from here, Miss Livvy." Amos elbowed between Heath and the counter. "Out of the way, newbie. I'll fix it since you don't have the kitchen instinct God gave a goose."

Without measuring a thing, the older man upended bottles of strange seasonings, dropped chunks of butter and added streams of milk to the bowl. After a couple minutes of stirring with a huge spoon till he was red in the face, Amos swiped a taste and pronounced it *passable*.

"It's time for me to go help in the dining room." He handed the spoon to Heath. "Clean up over here, and then see if you can figure out how to open those plastic bags and put the rolls in the bread baskets. And try not to make any more mess than you already have, ya pig." Amos jerked his head toward the potato-spattered countertop before he stomped from the room.

Heath slanted a questioning look at Olivia who shrugged in response.

"I admitted up front I don't have any experience," Heath explained, then turned to Bruce. "My mother didn't like me in her way while she was cooking."

"Is there a chance you ever insulted your mama while she was fixin' you a meal?" Bruce asked. "'Cause that might explain why she didn't want your company in her kitchen. Same goes for Amos."

"Huh?" Heath hadn't slept more than a few hours in a row for a couple of weeks, thanks to a stakeout where the good guys had come up nearly empty-handed. He was exhausted and asked to delay this assignment until tomorrow. But Biddle insisted that Heath get on the case right away, and without any of the disguises he normally used during undercover operations. He'd been told to report as is, clean-faced and bare-headed, a situation he'd never encountered before.

The confusion just kept on piling up. He strained his brain to understand the comparison Bruce had just made between Heath's mama and Amos. Obviously he'd done something wrong. "Are you saying I insulted the guy?"

"When you came into the kitchen with Miss Livvy we heard what you said about *sir* being code for *feeble old geezer.* When you called Amos *sir* two beats later, I thought that big vein on the side of his neck might explode."

"I was simply showing respect," Heath explained.

"You can't have it both ways. Everything's black and white with Amos."

Heath looked to Olivia, who nodded agreement.

He hung his head. How he wished for a beard and horn-rimmed glasses to hide his naked face. There was comfort beneath camouflage. Being out in the world like this made him feel exposed.

Judged.

The real Heath Stone wasn't exactly a guy people took to right away. And who could blame them?

Most days Heath didn't even like himself.

"Oh, don't worry too much about it," Olivia said, cutting him a break. "It may take a while, but Amos will warm up to you once he gets to know you."

"How long you plan to stay?" Bruce asked. A smirk twisted one corner of his mouth. "I've been here three months and he's still calling me Bryan."

"Well, *Bryan,*" Olivia picked up the joke, "things are under control in here so how about checking with Velma to see if she needs help? With these freezing temps I expect a full-capacity night."

Bruce nodded, scrapped his pile of chopped vegetables into a container and stored it in an oversized fridge. He hung his apron over a peg on the way out of the kitchen.

"Sorry I got off to a bad start," Heath felt he should apologize, though he wasn't sure he'd done anything so awful.

"Most people have the same experience with Amos." Olivia tore big sheets of tin foil from a roll mounted on the wall and tucked them over the giant bowl of mashed potatoes.

"Including you?" Heath grabbed paper towels and began to clean up the mess he'd made.

When she didn't respond right away, he glanced up. He was captivated for the second time that hour by the fair skin that rose above the neck of her sweater and the short crop of jet-black hair framing her face. Something quickened inside Heath's chest at the thought of this woman being guilty of trafficking drugs, especially if it was to support her thieving father who'd fled the country a decade earlier to avoid prosecution for tax evasion. The Feds had never given up on finding Dalton Wyatt and they wondered if he might somehow be behind the recent influx of meth and ecstasy that seemed to be passing through this shelter.

Heath watched tiny lines crinkle the corners of Olivia's indigo eyes, where she squinted as if the answer to his question was a pleasant memory.

"God's touch was all over my first encounter with Amos." The event was a sweet memory for Olivia. "We hit it off right away. He needed a place to live and I needed someone I could depend on."

"What about your family?" Heath dipped his chin and turned his attention to wiping down the countertop.

"I've been on my own since high school,

so help from family hasn't been an option for years."

She wondered how his life compared to hers. Wondered if he could possibly understand what it was like to be alone in the world, not knowing whether you'd have food to eat or a roof over your head from one day to the next. Heath Stone spent his life sitting at a computer while she went door-to-door asking for donations to feed the hungry. They probably didn't have much in common at all.

Still, she'd been asked by Detective Biddle to let Heath repay his debt to the community through service at her mission. Maybe the time he spent at Table of Hope would have a life-changing impact. Maybe he'd find even more than anyone expected.

Chapter Two

Olivia watched Heath throughout the meal. He was obviously uncomfortable having his dinner in a shelter. He avoided eye contact, ate with his head down. He kept his elbows pulled close to his body, careful not to brush against his neighbors as if that would keep their cooties away.

The guy was definitely out of place among the homeless but after the strained introductions in the kitchen she suspected he might never find his personal comfort zone.

Anywhere.

Though Detective Biddle had briefly shared the circumstances that cost Heath a hundred hours of community service, she knew nothing about him personally. Was he a political activist or just a prankster? What on earth had compelled him to make the trip over from his home in Austin, visit the public library in Waco and use his talent to break into the city's computer system? Whatever his objective, the price of reaching it had been high. The court had slapped Heath with the maximum number of hours and threatened him with contempt if he left Waco without serving his full sentence. They'd even impounded his vehicle!

If not for the creative thinking of Detective Biddle, Heath could be working highway detail during the coldest year on record. From the hangdog expression on his face he might actually prefer the road crew to eating in her cozy dining hall and sleeping in the men's quarters for a while.

A shoulder nudged playfully against Olivia's.

"Ain't he somethin', just like I said?" Velma whispered.

"Would you stop!" Olivia hissed, hiding the humor that would only encourage her friend.

"Mmm, mmm, mmm," Velma smacked her always-painted lips. "That man needs a lady friend and I just might have to apply for the job, even if it's only part-time."

As Olivia stood to clear her plate from the table, she gave Velma's arm a pinch. "You behave yourself," she instructed. "We have rules here and for good reason."

Even so, it was impossible to disagree with

Velma's assessment. Heath's questioning brown eyes had met Olivia's only once across the table. For the brief seconds she'd held his gaze, a deep sense of emptiness had stirred in her spirit. Olivia wasn't experienced enough with relationships to know if the need she recognized was his or her own.

As she carried her plate toward the cleanup station, she tried to imagine what Heath thought of her cheerfully painted dining hall. She sniffed the warm air, wrinkled her nose. Okay, it got a bit smelly in the evenings with all the food and the crowd of people right off the street. But before lights out everyone would have an opportunity to freshen up, to appreciate a brief shower.

The hot water heaters would be nearly empty by the time the staff had a turn. But with a man as handsome as Heath Stone as their new resident, the chill of a cold shower was probably a good idea. Especially for Velma!

If Heath added up all the dishes he'd washed in his twenty-nine years of life, it would still be less than the number of plates that passed through his sink tonight. He was fairly sure this would become a frequent event, so he needed to accomplish the job he'd been sent to do and then make tracks toward a new future in a new place.

Just today he'd firmly decided to leave the force.

"I gotta get out of drug enforcement, Biddle," Heath had complained to his trusted friend at lunchtime over chips and vending machine sandwiches. "What's the use in bustin' college kids for dime bags when there's an endless supply out there? It's just a waste of effort and tax dollars."

"Oh, come on," Biddle chuckled. "It was a bigger deal than that. You're just sufferin' post-stakeout blues. You say this every time a case wraps and you have to cool your heels waitin' on the grand jury."

Bill Biddle was patient to a fault when a cop needed to let off steam. Venting had become a daily occurrence for Heath, frustrated as he was by the constant stream of drugs across the Mexican border into Texas.

"It would be different if the indictments paid off," Heath griped. "But the honcho of this new outfit seems to have an endless supply of product and every money-grubbin' lawyer in Texas in his hip pocket. Living in disguise twenty hours a day is making it harder and harder to remember who I am. It's just not worth it to me anymore."

"Listen, son." Biddle had laced his fingers across a sixty-something belly. "I know going undercover wasn't your first career choice, but you're good at the work. Stick with us till we can afford another full-timer in the Computer Crimes Unit. Microsoft and Google aren't the only places a natural nerd can find his calling, you know."

Heath reached for another dirty plate, grateful for the ugly yellow gloves that were a barrier between him and cleaning up after these homeless people. This place was definitely not for him and the sooner he was out from under the eagle eye of Grandpa Amos, the better.

Earlier, while Heath picked up the shattered pieces of a fumbled cup, he'd foolishly mentioned that using disposable stuff might be a good idea. He was swiftly educated about the virtues of soap, water and elbow grease versus garbage that would still be in a landfill when Christ returned. Then Amos started in about the number of trees that died for the sake of paper plates when a restaurant supply had donated perfectly good dishes.

"And, by the way, butterfingers," he'd warned, "try not to break anything else. Money's tight around here!"

Olivia's return to the kitchen was like a sedative, quieting the curmudgeon who was a cranky

Pit Bull guarding his boss lady's business. As she picked up a stack of clean bowls near Heath's work area and then stepped away, a sweet aroma lingered. She turned to carry them to the dish pantry and he seized the moment.

"Um, excuse me. Could we talk?"

"Sure," she answered. A patient smile lifted the corners of her tired eyes. Setting the bowls back on the counter, she grabbed a fresh kitchen towel to dry the coffee cups in his drainer. The woman's hands hadn't been still since she'd introduced herself. He knew rookie cops who could use a dose of her stamina.

"It's been crazy here tonight," she admitted. "That's the nature of a shelter in the winter. When the weather's warm, folks leave right after the meal, but if it's freezing we tend to bed down almost everybody. And even when it finally gets quiet, there still seem to be a dozen problems that need attention."

"I noticed." He'd only been in the place a few hours and had already come to the conclusion there must be easier ways to get some of the jobs done. But if it was all a front for drugs, why care about efficiency?

"So, what can I do for you?" she asked.

Before he bothered to state his case, Heath was pretty sure what the woman standing beside him would say, but he needed an opportunity to poke around the place when everybody else would be occupied. He gave it a shot.

"You can tell me Amos is wrong about nightly Bible study being a requirement of staying here."

Olivia flung her red checkered towel over her left shoulder and pointed to a plaque on the wall above their heads. It was identical to the one he'd noticed above the front entrance.

Seek ye first the Kingdom of God, and His righteousness; and all these things shall be added unto you. Matthew 6:33

"We're in the business of seeking God. Shelter and food are only the physical part of what Table of Hope is about. Introducing lost souls to Christ and helping believers grow closer to Him is the primary reason we're here. If you're going to be with us even for a short while, worship is non-negotiable. It's a daily time that brings the staff together with a common heart."

"But what if I don't believe that stuff anymore? Why would you want me to take part if I didn't feel the same way you do?"

"Faith comes by hearing the message and the message comes through the Word of God. Just because you don't feel the same way I do doesn't mean the Holy Spirit can't use Scripture to meet your needs, whatever they are."

Heath's jaw tightened, sending a pinpoint of pain into his temple. This shouldn't be a big deal. He'd find another way to skin this cat. But having somebody force religion on him rankled all the same, reminded him of the well-meaning adoptive parents who were forever trying to suck him into their church activities. Once they moved to Florida, he thought this sort of coercion was behind him.

Evidently not.

"I'll cooperate because I have to, just like I have to wash dishes." Heath reached for more dirty flatware and slid spoons and forks into the sudsy water while keeping his gaze away from the intensity of Olivia's oh-so-lovely eyes. "But I want to say up front that requiring me to listen to Bible study will be about as effective as forcing me to do community service. Neither one can rehabilitate the person I am inside."

A hand rested lightly on his shoulder. His already tense muscles stiffened more.

"Is it being stuck here that's got you keyed up or are you angry at the world in general?"

"Is submitting to therapy also a requirement of your program?" He glanced at the spot where her fingers touched him, warming the flesh beneath the fabric of his long-sleeved shirt.

Olivia pulled her hand away. She reached for another dish and continued to help in spite of his rudeness.

"May I ask what kind of work you do in Austin?"

"Government security." He began to spin a fresh web of lies, making up his story as he went along. Saying whatever it took to get her to drop her guard.

"Will you lose your job over this?"

It was natural for Heath to examine the motives behind questions. Did this lady really care what happened to him? Could her ministry to this captive audience be sincere, or was this God business just a more intricate cover than the average dope dealer bothered to set up? A loyal daughter would go to a lot of trouble to protect her father, even if he didn't deserve it.

Heath turned his head, his eyes searching hers. He smiled to mask his suspicions.

"One of Waco's city officials is the brother of my boss. He challenged me to hack into their Intranet just to stick it to his brother. I actually did the city a favor by pointing out the weakness in their network, but the mayor didn't see it that way. Even though I didn't access anything confidential, Judge Wapner still threw the book at me. I covered for my boss and he's letting me use vacation time till I get home."

"Do you have family in Austin?"

"Nope." Heath said the word like punctuation to end the prying.

Olivia caught the hint, knew he was telling her to back off, but she kept pressing. "So it was a security job that drew you to our state capital?"

If this guy thought she'd go away easily, he had another think coming. People were her life's work. Each one had a story worth telling and most needed somebody to listen. Maybe if she'd been tuned in to her father, she'd have recognized the signs of trouble, spotted the depth of his deception before it was too late.

But she'd barely been nineteen back then. He'd run like a coward and left her alone to face the enormity of his white collar crime. His disgraceful departure devastated Olivia. He left her with nothing but the landmark family home that was her late mother's inheritance, Olivia's birthright. Selling off the antiques kept the taxes paid and the water turned on, but little more. Once the place was nearly empty, it only made sense to let the property go and use what funds were left to do something positive to restore the Wyatt name by giving back to the community her father had swindled.

Some citizens had objected to another mission, even complained that it encouraged transients to frequent the area. Olivia would not be distracted by opposition, since she realized from her first volunteer experience that she was called to witness to the homeless. Or nonbelievers like the one standing before her now with his rubber gloves fisted on his hips.

"Is this an interview?" Even while he was glaring and demanding an answer, the man was a pleasant sight. His lean arms pulled the sleeves of his black T-shirt tight against a solid chest. "Or are you just nosy with everybody?"

"Pretty much everybody, but especially with the ones I allow to hang around for a while," she said, a reminder that she had every right to ask a few questions. "Some of your answers would already be in writing for me if you'd had time to fill out the paperwork. How about if I empty out that sink while you take a break and get those forms completed."

The glare of his eyes softened, the set of his jaw seemed to relax and his head tilted ever so slightly as if he were sizing her up. He turned back to the sink and resumed his attack on the white stoneware.

"If you get a nonnegotiable, then so do I."

Olivia detected a hint of humor in his words. "And what would that be?"

"I don't shy away from hard work. I pull my own weight, especially in the service of a lovely lady."

She hadn't thought of herself as a *lady* in quite a long time, let alone one who was lovely. Humility was a free by-product of dressing in cast-off clothes.

"I never argue with a man who wants to do his part." She sidestepped the compliment. People were generally grateful when you took them in, so it was her practice not to read too much into flattery.

"Miss Livvy, a toilet in the women's lavatory is overflowin' like the Brazos in rainy season." Velma stood in the doorway with a mop in one hand and a janitor's bucket at her side.

"Not again," Olivia groaned. "The plumber promised it was fixed."

"I already shut the pipes off, but I could use some help to clean up the water."

"I got it." Heath made a beeline for Velma and relieved her of the mop. "Point the way."

"Just follow the stream." She glanced at the wet tile floor. "It'll lead you straight to the source."

"You get the ladies out?"

"Sure did."

"Can you wait by the door till I give the all-clear signal? We wouldn't want anybody to slip and fall."

"I got you covered, sugar cookie." Velma winked at Olivia before she hurried after Heath.

Olivia offered up a prayer of thanks for having another pair of strong hands for a while, whether he was a willing volunteer or not. He hadn't hesitated to take charge of cleanup in the ladies' room, a place most guys wouldn't go if their lives depended on it. He even made it a one-man job, so maybe that would get a thumbs-up from Amos. Staff relationships were important in close quarters.

She'd been exposed to a lot of unhappy people in her life and Heath had a thorn in his paw, for sure. If she had to make an educated guess, she'd say it had more to do with how he felt about himself than how he felt about the world around him.

According to Detective Biddle, Heath had thought about it for a while before choosing Table of Hope for his community service. She understood his reluctance to move into a shelter. Lots of people break the law intentionally, but very few associate with homeless folks by choice. A mission wasn't exactly one step up from a labor camp and serving others shouldn't be considered as a form of punishment.

Still, she'd gone along with the arrangement because it was nice to know Waco's finest were aware and keeping an eye on activity at the shelter. There was a modicum of comfort in knowing that she wasn't totally on her own when the lights went out each night. With so few trustworthy men in her life, the cops were high on her short list.

Chapter Three

A quick search of the women's hot pink locker room for evidence to pin on Olivia Wyatt left Heath empty-handed. But he really hadn't expected to find anything incriminating, at least not that easily. So he tackled the wet floor, pushing and pulling the industrial-size mop across the linoleum, pausing every few sloppy strokes to squeeze the head in the wringer attached to the bucket. As he worked, he mulled over his situation. For some reason he felt even more bent out of shape than usual.

"What's your problem, Stone?" he grumbled aloud. "Just do the drill and get out. This assignment is a cakewalk compared to the last one."

Five days ago he'd been in full body armor, a stinger in his grip, as he used the steel battering ram to break down the door of a crack house. A cop could never be sure what he'd find on the other side; could be drug-dazed kids, could be gunfire.

Hanging out at Table of Hope would be a big honkin' bore by comparison. But hadn't he just tried to convince Biddle that a quiet existence was exactly what the doctor ordered? Putting his life on the line over drugs was a losing battle. As soon as he wrapped this case he'd be off to the West Coast and the life of a professional geek.

"You 'bout done?" Velma yelled through an inch-wide crack in the door. "I got ladies who need to get in there."

"You tell 'em unless they want to slip on this wet floor and break a leg to hold their horses for ten more minutes," Heath yelled back. Then he muttered, "Pushy woman."

"I heard that," Velma called as the door creaked shut.

He felt a smile spread the width of his face, maybe for the first time in days. This place was definitely run by control freaks, but that seemed to be a good thing. From what he'd been able to observe, the facility was clean and in spite of his lame contribution to the meal, the food had been tasty and plentiful. It was a good thing since there were more hungry and homeless around here than he'd have guessed.

Yep, with so many people coming and going and the staff's constant activity, this shelter would make a convenient cover for drug trafficking whether Olivia was involved or not.

Olivia.

He was bugged by a quality in her that he couldn't quite identify. Was she a willing participant, covering for someone who'd let her take the fall? Or was she the real deal with this religious stuff? There was softness in Olivia's dark gaze that appeared ready to forgive unknown and unconfessed sins. It was reckless and brave at the same time and, again, difficult to interpret.

He found that as worrisome as an unchained guard dog. Heath's knack for reading people made him good at his job, kept him alive. Olivia Wyatt would be a challenge. Well, at least he'd leave undercover work on an interesting note, thanks to the unconventional nature of this assignment.

He crushed the mop in the wringer while reviewing the personal decision he'd admitted to Biddle earlier that day. Heath's mind was made up. He was ready to nail shut the pine box on this phase of his life, bury the work he'd been doing in an unmarked grave and move across the country. Short of going into witness protection, this was the only way to move on with his life.

Anyone closely associated with Heath was in danger if the criminals he'd sent to jail ever put two and two together. He wasn't afraid for himself but concern for his parents was the reason he'd bought out their duplex and hurried them off to an early retirement in sunny Florida. The hurt in their voices when he refused their offers to visit during holidays was slowly choking an already weak relationship.

All Heath's life, his folks had been perplexed by his sullen personality and working under-cover only magnified his skepticism. Every day he moved further away from being the son they wanted, the son they deserved. This was not a life worth sharing and it was the very reason he didn't dare reconnect with his biological sisters.

Heath hadn't been much more than a toddler when the mother he couldn't recall was murdered at the hands of their brutal father, sending two daughters and a son into the family court system to be scattered like wildflower seeds in a Texas whirlwind. He'd found an adoptive home, but nobody had wanted the older girls, Alison and Erin.

Twenty-five years later, Alison had some-how found his address and tried repeatedly to make contact. Her most recent letter was still in his backpack. He didn't have the heart to write *Return to Sender* on another envelope.

The woman was a stranger, but she was still his sister and deserved his protection. He knew very little about her, she knew nothing about him, and as things stood today it had to stay that way.

He clenched his jaw as he acknowledged the key to his anger. It wasn't so much the constant battle with criminals as it was the by-product, his growing anonymity. The past six years had taught Heath to be invisible, and he was tired of living like a phantom. He wanted his life back. He wanted to know his family.

"That's what's bugging me!" Heath said to himself, the revelation suddenly clear as he pushed the mop across the floor.

The thought struck him like a gun butt to the skull. Olivia Wyatt was the only thing standing between Heath and his future. As soon as this case was solved, he could move on with his life.

He'd crack that unreadable expression and get her to show her true colors no matter what it took. And he'd start right now.

Heath's gaze swept the nearly dry floor, coming to rest on the row of lockers. His fingers twitched at the thought of rifling behind the doors that were padlocked. The men's private area would look just like this, which meant there were at least fifty locks to pick. He had the tools and experience to give it a go, but time was his enemy. There was no telling what else in the place was kept under lock and key. With a transient clientele, that probably meant everything of value.

Female voices grumbled in the hallway.

"All clear!" he called. The door burst open with Velma, a red-lipped fireplug of a woman in the lead and a dozen more close behind.

"It's about time." She leaned her hip against the open door and held it wide for him to exit. "The kitchen is closed up for the night so grab your Bible and meet us in the big room. Miss Livvy's expecting you."

Before he could comment that he didn't own a Bible and had no idea where to find the big room, the line of women had shuffled past him, headed toward the showers.

"Last one gets cold water," Velma explained as the door closed in his face.

Heath stood alone in the hallway, not at all sure which way to turn but certain somebody would give him bossy instructions at any moment. Meanwhile, he simply took a few beats to appreciate the floor-to-ceiling strokes of color that brought the walls of the corridor to life.

Lavish green plants and a rainbow of flowers sprang from soil you would swear was damp from rain. Birds of yellow and scarlet perched on shaded limbs of tall trees. A lazy blue stream wound through the setting, splashing down layers of rock and over smooth stones. Sunny rays filtered through clouds casting shadows that swayed with the wind. The scene was breathing with primary colors but mostly it was…moving. Alive with motion.

He stared hard, shook his head. He really needed a good night's rest.

Olivia turned a corner and headed Heath's way. "You like?" She swept her hand toward the walls.

"I can't believe I hardly noticed it the first time I passed through here," he confessed.

"Yeah, you really have to stand still and take it in. Eventually, everything starts to move. It's kinda creepy in the dark but still cool."

Heath nodded, glad it wasn't the lack of sleep getting the better of him. But this kind of talent had to be expensive. He spotted an opportunity, baited the trap.

"I'm surprised you can afford art like this on the tight budget Amos keeps reminding me about. It must have cost a small fortune."

She waved away Heath's concern. "Oh, the paint is donated and I do all the work myself."

"*You're* the artist?" Heath stared again at the walls.

"Oh, I don't know about being an artist, but I do all the painting around here. I had some help with the exterior, but I did the inside by myself before we opened."

Heath couldn't recall another day in his life when he'd been caught off guard so many times in such a brief period. Either this woman was something special or he was slipping.

Whatever the answer turned out to be, it was just a job. A job standing between him and the rest of his life.

"I came to get you for Bible study," Olivia explained.

"It's been a long day. Can't I get a pass since it's my first night here?"

"Nice try, but I already saved you a seat up front." A smirk lifted one corner of her mouth. "Right next to Amos."

Heath was mesmerized by Olivia as she spoke to the small group. She perched on a folding chair in the common space they called the big room, sitting tall with one foot tucked beneath her. For half an hour she talked about the Book of Job in a way that made the man's struggles come to life, like the scenes she'd painted on the walls in the hallway.

Until that moment Heath had viewed Job merely as one more character from the stories he'd been told during childhood. Noah built his ark, Moses parted the Red Sea and Lazarus returned from the dead. Those were little more than fairy tales to Heath. Still, he loved a good superhero.

But Olivia was presenting a flesh-and-blood man whose trust in God overcame the worst trials Satan had up his sleeve. She made a convincing argument for faith and it was tempting to buy into her perspective.

Heath would keep that in mind. Charisma was an excellent shield. The world was full of smooth-talking leaders with hidden agendas. A disapproving puff of air rushed past Heath's lips at the aggravating thought.

The point of an elbow poked against his ribs. Amos's scowl indicated that Heath should bow his head, somebody was praying. He dipped his chin but slanted his eyes toward the others. He recognized a few faces from dinner, when he'd kept mostly to himself. During the meal he'd risked a glance across the room at Olivia. Her eyes were already fixed on him, affirming what he expected; she was keeping him under scrutiny.

And she should. He was a stranger, new on her turf, and as far as she knew he'd been convicted of a cyber crime. Yet he hadn't seen any judgment in her eyes, only kindness.

The closing prayer droned on, so Heath's gaze wandered back to the front of the room and homed in on Olivia. As if he'd tapped her on the shoulder, she looked up, gave him a brief smile and lowered her eyelids again.

"Shame on you," Amos hissed when the meeting was dismissed.

"For what?"

"For lookin' around when Bruce was praying."

"If you'd been minding your own business you wouldn't have noticed."

"I was just checkin' to make sure you were participating."

"I agreed to attend. I never said I'd participate."

"That's true." Olivia came to his rescue. "Heath is meeting all the requirements and he's done an okay job." She looked his way, her eyes wide with expectation. "So far."

"It must be tough to get an *atta boy* around here," he mumbled.

Olivia watched a sullen glaze settle in Heath's eyes, like that of a brooding boy who longed for approval.

"Well, it's a bit soon for praise, don't you think? Give me a few days to see how you fold laundry and make beds."

Heath's shoulders slumped forward. He shoved his fists deep into the pockets of his baggy jeans, hiding and folding in on himself in one motion.

Olivia couldn't wait to get his enrollment forms and study them in her personal quarters upstairs, the only truly private area of the shelter. Something was up with this guy and she planned to figure it out during the time he'd be completing his community service.

"Come on, sugar cookie." Velma appeared at Heath's side. "I'll show you the rest of the place."

"I'll take over from here," Olivia was firm. She looked from Velma to Amos. "I need the two of you to get a final head count before we lock up for the night."

"Alrighty, then." Velma fanned her fingers in a goodbye and tugged at Amos's sleeve to ensure that he was close behind.

"Thanks for joining us this evening." Olivia acknowledged Heath's presence in her Bible study.

"I didn't think I had a choice."

"You didn't. But you attended without an argument and that's appreciated."

"Do you get much backtalk?"

Olivia couldn't hold in a smile. The guy seemed clueless about the streets. Maybe his tough look was all for show and he really was a nerd in skater boy clothing after all.

"What's so funny?" His brows drew together.

She motioned toward the coffee station and moved away from the conversation couches of the big room. She poured a cup and turned her back to the others as she offered it to Heath.

"Homeless folks can be unpredictable." She kept her voice low. "Sometimes they're so worn down by their circumstances that there's no fight left. It's all they can do to put one foot in front of the other each day looking for shelter and food. Other times they're like cheap firecrackers. The fuse is already short and it's just a matter of time before they explode.

"And, sadly, we get our fair share of clients with mental problems. We do the best we can, referring folks where better resources can meet their needs."

He nodded. "So, if nobody melts down or blows a gasket it's a good day."

"That's it in a nutshell." Olivia tore off several sheets from the wall-mounted paper towel dispenser and began wiping up drips and splashes around the coffee urn.

Heath leaned against the wall, crossed his arms, shook his head. "Isn't there a smarter way for a single lady to make a living? I mean, where's your chance for advancement, your five-year plan?"

"Thoughtful questions from a guy spending

his vacation in a homeless shelter because he was too shortsighted to consider the consequences of a prank against city government."

Olivia couldn't resist dishing it right back when Heath had the nerve to question the wisdom of her professional decisions.

"My bad." Heath lowered his eyes, tapped the toe of his sneaker against the linoleum of the big room.

Was hanging his handsome head a sign of humility? Or shame? Or just an act?

Olivia planned to figure out which one it was but she didn't need to get in a hurry. Heath still had about ninety-five hours left on his sentence, plenty of time for her to decide what made him tick.

Chapter Four

Even though Heath's question could have been posed more diplomatically, he'd been straightforward in the asking. He deserved an honest response, and he was watching Olivia now with expectation in his brown eyes.

"You're not the first person to inquire about my ambitions," she noted in response. "As a matter of fact I had to justify myself to the zoning commission and then again to some local churches who give us financial support. Table of Hope is my calling, but it's also my sole responsibility."

"I heard your father funded this place."

Her hands stilled, her gaze met his.

"Is that supposed to be some kind of cruel joke?"

He pushed away from the wall, stood tall. "No, and I'm sorry 'cause I can see I've offended you. Detective Biddle said you were the boss lady and

I thought he mentioned something about your father."

"He probably did." She closed her eyes for a moment, wondering if she'd ever break free of the past. "I forgot you're not from around here and you don't know the Wyatt family history."

She dropped to one knee to unlock the cabinet beneath the coffee bar. As she pulled the double doors wide, he moved closer and bent low to peer inside.

"Can I give you a hand with that?" Heath offered, his eyes glancing toward the contents of the storage shelves.

"Sure." She moved aside, gave him access. "This area needs to be restocked a couple of times a day with just enough for a few hours. We can't leave the supplies sitting out or they'll walk away."

"It's the same where I work. People on the honor system always develop sticky fingers."

"I'm afraid that's been my experience, too," she admitted.

"What happens if you catch somebody stealing?"

"We haven't had to face that situation yet, but I'd remind the person we require honesty and accountability for our supplies. The clients have to respect that if they want to remain at Table of Hope."

"A reminder is good, but removing temptation is still the best defense."

She nodded in agreement. "That's why we keep a close watch on our pantry and almost everything goes under lock and key at nine o'clock."

"Want me to close this back up for you?" He opened his palm. Olivia removed the keys from her neck and dropped them in his hand.

"It's the one with the black plastic tag, the same color as the dot beside the lock."

He stood, returned her keys. "So everything's color-coded?"

"You got it." She moved toward the door, motioned for Heath to follow as she headed for the check-in area. "I hope you're an early riser. The newest resident always gets the first shift."

"I don't sleep much, so that's no problem. Midnight to four is about the only rest I can count on. So sign me up for crack-of-dawn duty."

Passing into the front lobby, Olivia took the clipboard from Velma, blocking any chance for her to pounce on Heath. "Amos will love you for being an early bird."

"First he has to get over hating me for being clueless in the kitchen."

Olivia ignored the concern and motioned toward her office, a head-high cubicle that shielded a metal desk and two chairs.

"Amos is a wonderful person and I couldn't

get by without him." She felt the need to explain. "But he lost everything at an age when a man should be enjoying life. I hope we can turn it around over time, but he's become a glass-half-empty kinda guy."

"The last time I heard somebody use that term they were talkin' about me," Heath offered as he settled into her creaky desk chair.

"Would you agree that's true?"

"Pretty much."

"Doesn't that bother you?" Olivia pressed.

"Should it?" His head hitched to one side, a challenge in his eyes.

"I suppose not if you're okay with your perspective being defined by lack instead of abundance. It seems sad, choosing to limit your possibilities in life."

"I didn't say I was okay with it, but I can't help the way I'm hardwired," he insisted.

"Sorry, but I don't accept that excuse from you any more than I buy it from Amos. We may be predisposed to certain behaviors, but God gave us free will for a purpose. Every moment we're awake presents a new choice with different consequences. The pessimist's life is bound by doubt and doing without. James says we have not because we ask not. When we reach out to God with unselfish motives, He listens."

"You sound like my mother. She's always quoting the Bible."

"Then I'll take that as a compliment."

"It's a waste of time for her and it will be for you, too." He pushed the words through clamped teeth. "The day my folks moved to a retirement community was the day I was freed from their efforts to give me religion."

He lowered his eyes and his head, took up a pen and began scribbling answers on the questionnaire. The finality in Heath's words was like a blanket smothering the potential for fire in his spirit. Olivia's heart was sad for him.

Her own sainted mother had lost the battle with diabetes in her thirties. But in the fourteen precious years they'd had together Anne Wyatt faithfully discipled her only child, as if knowing Olivia would be alone one day, needing the Truth as her anchor.

And here this foolish man sat complaining about his mother's desire to give him a spiritual upbringing. Well, maybe he'd escaped the efforts of his parents, but for a short while anyway he'd be seated at Table of Hope where the glass was perpetually full because the Holy Spirit was always present.

Olivia watched him pressing pen to paper, probably giving as little information as possible. She'd check his answers first thing in the morning. As he wrote, she silently prayed for her personal witness to somehow have an impact on his heart. Heath hungered in a way that resonated more profoundly than a desperate client's need for food.

"Hand the clipboard to Velma when you're finished and she'll assign you to a bunk in the men's dorm and give you a welcome kit. That should get you through the night, and then we'll cover the rest in the morning."

Heath could tell from the determined set of Olivia's jaw that he'd just become her new cause. Good. That meant she'd stay close to him. She'd learn soon enough he was a lost cause, but that was her business. His business was to dig deep beneath the surface of this place and its owner until the core was exposed.

"So, that's it for tonight?" He tapped the pen against the metal clip on the board. He hadn't made much progress so far. "I thought you wanted to review my form?"

She cupped her right hand behind her neck, squeezing as she tipped her face forward. "That was my plan until my head started to throb a couple of minutes ago."

"I have that effect on people."

She raised her face, a tired smile in her eyes. "You get partial credit, but mostly I suspect the barometric pressure is dropping along with the temperature. I'm gonna call it a night, go upstairs and settle down with my favorite old quilt."

"Should I slip this under your door when I'm done?"

"Thanks for offering, but there's a locked stairwell between my apartment and the first floor of the shelter. A male resident always works the back exit and he keeps an eye on my entrance, too."

"It's smart you take precautions. A woman alone in this world needs to guard herself constantly."

"I volunteered and studied missions for years while I planned Table of Hope and I gave a lot of thought to my personal space. So don't worry about me." She locked her desk drawer and pushed out of her chair. "Get a good night's sleep because we have a busy day tomorrow."

She disappeared around the wall of the cubicle, then several seconds later poked her head back into view. "And I look forward to reading about your family so don't scrimp on the answers."

With Olivia out of sight and Heath alone behind the small desk, he smacked his palm against his forehead.

What on earth made me mention my parents? Now I have to make something up about them.

Or did he? This could be a golden opportunity

to test the waters, discover how it felt to be himself instead of some version he concocted as he went along. He pondered it for a moment. Nope, he shook his head. Not a good idea to start unearthing the truth when a lie worked perfectly well.

Heath's shoulders slumped lower as he accepted how easily fabricating a background came to him, along with each assignment. It seemed the obvious way to protect his real family history. He was the only child of adoptive parents, but he had two natural sisters out there who wanted their brother to be part of their lives. Considering it seriously had always been too risky. And how would he deal with it if his sisters turned out to be dominated and abused like their birth mother? Or worse, what if they were single-minded, Bible-verse-quoting women like the one who had just lectured him about his pessimistic attitude?

"Lord, I sure hope my sisters fall somewhere in the middle of those two extremes," Heath muttered.

"You need somethin' over there, sugar cookie?" Velma called across the panel.

"Sorry," he answered. "Just thinking out loud."

Hearing folks praying tonight must have dredged up that old habit of talking to God. What was it Olivia had said? *We have not because we ask not.* Heath had stopped asking for stuff a long time ago. It occurred to him that the comment Velma just overheard kinda resembled a prayer.

If God's likely to grant me a prayer request I should probably spend it on something of value, namely a good-paying job in Silicon Valley that lets me create software instead of lies.

Enough time wasted on introspection.

He was here to study Olivia Wyatt like the key to a final exam. He needed answers hidden somewhere in this building. They had to be uncovered before more college kids died. And before Heath could get on with his new life.

Chapter Five

❧

Just after 11:00 p.m. Heath figured out that a homeless shelter never completely goes to sleep for the night. Sure, the bunks were heavy with snoring figures and the lights were out in dorms and hallways. But the muted sounds of conversation, television, flushing, coughing and even someone softly singing continued to flow.

He wandered the halls, poking around in the few spaces that remained unlocked or unguarded. Heath was restless to search in earnest for clues leading to drug activity. Working on his own in a place that was perpetually active had him rethinking how long he might have to invest in this case.

At the front and back entrances, night shift residents sipped coffee and read, looking up each time he happened past.

"You need something?" The young man

who'd introduced himself as Nick paused over what appeared to be a textbook. He was seated at a folding table beside two doorways; one was clearly marked with an EXIT sign and the other, Heath assumed, led to the upstairs apartment.

"No, just antsy, I guess."

"First night at this shelter?"

"First night in *any* shelter," Heath admitted. "I'm here for community service. I guess I'll get used to it in a day or two."

Nick tucked a folded sheet of paper between the pages and closed his book. He motioned for Heath to take the other chair.

"I've been in and out of places like this for nearly two years," Nick shared. "I'm still not used to it. So don't be surprised if it never feels like home."

The kid was well-spoken. Heath pointed toward the thick volume. "You a student?"

"Only for a little longer." Nick grinned and nodded. "I was almost finished with technical school when I lost my job and apartment. I had to drop out, figured that was the end of my education. But since Table of Hope took me in I've been able to catch up. In a couple more months I'll graduate, be qualified for work and get back on my feet again. I just need to put some money in the bank."

"Your folks must be proud of you for finding

a way to get back on track." Heath returned the young man's smile.

Shaggy hair fell across Nick's brow when he shook his head. "They don't even know where I am. I messed up too often to go home again."

Heath could understand not wanting to feed at the family trough, but given the choice between shelter and pride he'd take the former. "So, let me get this straight. You chose being homeless over being humble?"

Nick took a sip from a smiley face mug as though he needed a moment to consider his response. "You ever been on the street?" he finally asked.

"Not in the way you mean," Heath admitted.

"It's more humbling than you can imagine. You never get past the shame of asking a stranger for a handout. You've seen those WILL WORK FOR FOOD signs, right?"

Heath nodded.

"Well, holding that sign is less embarrassing than hearing yourself say the words over and over again. I know some people see us as bums who just won't get a job, and for a handful that may be true. But my experience at shelters tells me otherwise. If it wasn't for Miss Livvy's Christian heart, everybody here tonight might be sleeping in a doorway, and it wouldn't be because they're too lazy or proud to work.

"Trust me, if all I had to do was eat some crow to get my mama to invite me back to her table again, I wouldn't hesitate. But my parents never read about the prodigal son. I'm grateful that Miss Livvy believes in helping folks get another chance, no matter what they've done."

Warmth stirred beneath Heath's breastbone. Was there any possibility the woman he was investigating was truly as beautiful inside as she was on the outside?

Did that kind of person even exist in the world today?

Olivia stood before her bathroom sink, tipped her face toward the ceiling and made a gurgling sound through a mouthful of salty water. Too many encounters with the day's blustery wind had left her with a raw throat and throbbing ears. Thank goodness for home remedies. She couldn't afford medical insurance, so anything less critical than a severed limb had to be handled out of her first aid kit.

Two aspirin and a cup of hot tea should do the trick.

She rinsed her mouth, finger-combed short hair that stuck up every which way and dragged a favorite old Baylor sweatshirt over her head for added warmth. She padded into her small kitchen and pried open the tea bag tin.

Empty.

"Oh, that's right," she muttered. "I used the last one this morning." Crawling back under the blankets would be the simple thing to do, but when had she ever taken the easy road? She scooped up her wad of keys and flipped on the stairwell light. At the bottom she poked her head out, hoping to get Nick's attention and ask for a favor. He was nowhere in sight.

"It figures," Olivia griped as she trudged toward the big room. She'd make quick work of pocketing some tea bags from the drink station and get back upstairs before she was seen.

She found the room silent and empty, lit only by a plug-in night-light near the coffee urn.

"Yes!" Olivia cheered quietly, then hurried across the floor and reached for the tea canister. The lid flipped open easily. She grasped a handful of the small bags, raised them to her nose and closed her eyes to appreciate the fragrance.

"Excuse me," a male voice rumbled in her ear.

Olivia gasped! Her eyelids flew wide in the dark room.

The terse baritone and the fist gripping her wrist sent a shock wave shivering through her body. She gawked for a split second at the shadowy place where a strong hand held her captive.

Her gaze raced upward to the man's face. Sober eyes loomed close to hers.

"I believe under these circumstances I'm supposed to remind you about honesty and accountability, showing respect for the supplies at Table of Hope."

"And I believe under these circumstances I oughta have you skinned alive, Heath Stone. You scared the daylights out of me." She attempted and failed a defense training move to break his hold on her arm. "Let me go!" she hissed.

He squeezed harder and gave her a slight shake.

"Pay attention for a minute," his voice was insistent.

She stopped struggling, propped her free hand on her hip. "Okay, you have exactly sixty seconds before I call Detective Biddle to have you removed from my place."

"Fair enough, but listen. That little twist thing you just did with your arm might work with someone who's not expecting you to fight back. But you need to learn more aggressive tactics if you intend to hold your own against an attacker who won't give up easily."

He talked her though a judo maneuver that would put a man flat on his back and knock the wind out of him, giving her precious seconds to run for help.

"Now, *that's* what you need to do the next time a guy grabs you by the wrist."

"Dumping somebody on the floor that hard is cruel." She doubted she could be so brutal to another human being.

"Exactly! Always think of your own safety first. No man has the right to put his hands on a woman without her permission."

"The way you just did, you mean?" She rubbed the skin below her shirtsleeve.

"That was only to make an important point."

"Do you frequently make this point with women?"

"I've never shown that self-defense move to another person."

"Not even to your own mother?" Olivia asked.

Heath's expression went blank. He inhaled and exhaled before responding. "My mother's been dead for twenty-seven years."

Ten minutes later Olivia was seated on one of the big room's sofas at a right angle to Heath's chair. Her furry slippers were propped on the edge of a secondhand occasional table, and both hands cradled a mug of strong, hot tea. She should have made the time to retrieve his chart from the office, but the Holy Spirit was urging her to seize this moment and make it more personal, less about business.

"I'm not sure what possessed me to say that because I rarely think of my birth mother."

Olivia watched Heath cross one ankle over the other knee, jiggling his support leg in time with some cadence only he could hear. She'd seen the gesture before in applicants who were nervous. Or lying.

"Well, she was on your mind for some reason. Wanna tell me about her? I apologize if it seems like I'm prying, but as long as we're sitting here together at midnight we might as well get acquainted."

"Or I could show you another judo throw," he joked. The most mischievous grin Olivia had ever seen on a male over the age of eight dimpled Heath's cheeks. This handsome man must have been an adorable-looking child.

"I'll take you up on that offer in a few days when I'm feeling at the top of my game. Tonight the only thing I'm going to throw is a soggy tea bag if you don't tell me something about yourself."

His leg stopped jostling. He stared at the cup in his hands.

"When I was a toddler both of my parents were killed in an accident."

"Oh," Olivia pressed three fingers to her lips to contain a gasp. "I'm so sorry, Heath."

"I wasn't more than a baby, so I don't have any memories of them. It's not like I'm emotionally scarred or anything. But they didn't leave a will and nobody in the family could take me, so I was eventually adopted."

"Still, that's a terrible loss for a child no matter what the circumstances. How long have you known this?"

"Since middle school when my folks thought they should tell me the few facts they had."

"Have you made contact with any family members of your birth parents?"

"No." He shook his head. "There's no reason why I should after all this time. If anybody cared about me, they'd have made an effort by now."

"Maybe it's as simple as not having your name."

"My name was never changed." His eyes were downcast. "When the Brysons adopted me, they just tacked their last name on the end. I dropped Bryson when I turned eighteen."

Her heart was heavy with sadness. His adoptive parents must have been crushed by such an action from their son. "May I speak frankly?"

"Go ahead." He seemed to accept whatever might be coming.

"You've only been here a few hours and I've already heard you mention resenting your parents' faith and now your rejection of their name.

Have you considered how terribly painful that must have been for the people who raised you as their own?"

Oh Father, how hurtful it must be when so many of Your beloved children do the same thing to You!

"Of course I have." Heath dropped his chin, not so much to look contrite as to indicate that he got the point. "Look, they're good, Christian folks and I show my gratitude the best way I can. But in all our years together we never saw eye-to-eye on anything important. So it didn't come as a great surprise when they told me about the adoption. All of a sudden our failure to connect kinda made sense."

Olivia sipped cautiously while she considered his revelation. This man was as confused and complicated as anybody she'd encountered in her social work career. He seemed to have everything going for him and nothing to show for it emotionally or relationally.

"I know what you're thinking," Heath insisted. "I'm beyond redemption."

"Nobody's that far gone, no matter what's in their past or how big their issues may seem. We serve a God of second chances. He forgives us when we truly repent. He always welcomes us back."

Heath gave a dismissive shake of his head. "I

have a hard time buying that logic, but I realize it's a big part of what makes the whole faith deal seem attractive. I can see where people like you would think God's forgiving and reliable. There's not much reason to challenge that kind of teaching when you grow up in a picture-perfect family."

Olivia didn't need to consider whether the moisture burning her eyes was brought on by the steam from her tea or the sarcasm in his tone.

"You're not the only person who hasn't lived a happily-ever-after life, you know. My mother died when I was fourteen and my father fled the country over tax evasion charges when I was nineteen. I woke up alone one morning and realized God was all I had, and that was the day I also understood He was all I needed. He would never leave me or forsake me. It sure was *attractive,* as you put it, to have one thing in my life that was reliable on all those nights when I was flat broke and alone in an empty house ashamed to show my face in this town."

Heath's normally complacent heart thumped as he watched color deepen the lines in Olivia's face. Her eyes gleamed with indignation. He had the strangest urge to pull this woman into his arms and hug her protectively until the painful memories of her youth faded. But the firm set of her jaw warned him to keep his distance. She was likely to practice that judo throw he'd just taught her if he got too close.

I pushed too far, too aggressively. But the job is what it is. I'm here to search and destroy, not rescue and recover. And this lady is not exactly a damsel in distress, anyway.

What if she made good on her threat to call Biddle? Yeah, so what? He was the one who'd decided that using a disguise wasn't necessary on this job. But Biddle didn't realize that Heath's alter-ego characters were comfortable inside their borrowed skin, able to wing it no matter what the circumstances.

Not so for the flesh-and-blood man who couldn't seem to get his stories straight. He'd just pulled that accident stuff out of thin air. With this new twist to his lies, he'd have to be careful not to slip up.

"Why'd you get quiet all of a sudden? No more profound wisdom to share with me?" Olivia was torqued.

He should apologize. Contrition always seemed to make ladies happy.

"I'm sorry," he made the effort with as few words as possible.

"For what?" She wasn't gonna let him off the hook. Her heels may have been propped up on the coffee table, but Heath could sense the mental tapping of her toe as she waited for his answer. She tipped her head to the right and glared his way.

A few hours ago, in the last light of day, he'd thought her eyes were dark. In this shadowy room they were chunks of coal framed by extraordinary fair skin that any man in his right mind would reach out and touch.

On second thought, a guy had to be crazy to mess with such an angry woman. And Heath was feeling a little left of sane at the moment.

Chapter Six

"Well?" she demanded. "Exactly what is it that you're sorry for?" She reminded him of his weak apology.

"Evidently you have something in mind, so why don't you tell me?" he improvised.

"Let me see." She tapped her index finger to her chin, pretending to consider her response. "You should be sorry for shooting your mouth off without having the facts. And you should be ashamed of yourself for focusing on what's lacking in your life when you have such abundance to be thankful for. And don't even get me started on the foolishness that landed you in here when there are so many important things you could be doing with your time."

"You hit the mark on all counts." He held his hands up in surrender. "I offered you a potshot and you fired with both barrels."

Regret softened the squint of her eyes. "Okay, maybe that was too much."

"Nope, not at all." He shook his head. Her words were familiar. "It's not far from what my mom would have said, so I suppose I had it coming."

"There's that parallel between me and your mother again. You've made it clear y'all didn't see eye-to-eye on much, so I'm thinkin' that doesn't bode well for you and me."

"My mom and I disagree a lot but I respect her, just as I respect you for what you're doing with this place." He swept an open palm toward the room.

"And there's a lot more to do tomorrow." Olivia stood, the mug cupped between her hands and held close as if she had a chill. "So, I'm going to get some sleep and I suggest you do the same. Remember, you've got predawn duties."

"Yeah, Velma gave me the list. I think I can figure it all out on my own."

"You won't be alone. I'll be down first thing to give you a hand."

"You mean to keep an eye on me, don't you?"

A wry smile curved her pink lips. Her fingers fluttered a goodbye wave and she shuffled toward the door on fuzzy slippers.

* * *

"Don't look so surprised." Olivia acknowledged Heath's wide eyes as he entered the kitchen not very many hours later. "I told you I'd be down early."

"Yeah, but *early* is daylight. This is still the middle of the night." He pointed to the big round wall clock. It was just after 4:00 a.m.

She continued to punch out biscuits and place the soft dough on huge baking sheets while the ovens heated up.

"I had a stuffy head and thought it might clear up faster if I got out of bed."

Heath slid a fresh apron over his head and tied the strings behind his back. The man was attractive even at this gosh-awful hour, and suiting up for kitchen duty made him doubly appealing. Olivia checked her image in the blurry reflection in the glass of the wall-mounted oven. The flour that coated her hands also smudged her face, and scarecrow hair poked out from beneath the elastic of her hairnet.

"You remind me of a high school cafeteria lady," he teased.

"I was just thinking the same thing." She returned his grin and wondered when she'd totally stopped making an effort about her appearance.

"Do I need one of those?" His eyes glinted as he smiled and pointed toward her white nylon cap.

She slanted a glance his way that acknowledged he'd had his fun. "It's not required, but I try to set a good example for the kitchen help who have any hair to speak of."

"Where would you like me to get started?"

A puff of flour danced in the air as she waved toward the dining area. "Get coffee perking and make sure the sideboard is set with clean plates and utensils. Breakfast starts at five and you'll be amazed how many people will eat and get out the door as soon as the sun's up."

"Really? They don't want to hang around inside where it's warm?"

"Not an option." She shook her head. "Unless there's a weather crisis, everybody but the residents have to be out by eight o'clock so we can get started on our day."

"Get started? What do you call this?"

"This is what I call quiet time. Enjoy it while it lasts."

Two hours later Olivia signaled across the room for Heath to join her. She placed a basket of hot biscuits, fresh from the oven, and a jar of jelly on the table before settling into a chair. As Heath took the opposite seat, her stomach rumbled in a very unladylike way.

"Sounds like you took a breakfast break just in time." He offered her the basket and then put two on his own plate.

She placed a hand over her tummy, willing it to quiet down. "I was hoping you hadn't noticed."

"How could I miss something that loud?" He stabbed a pat of butter. "It was either your stomach or a diesel truck."

"I guess we're not even going to pretend to be polite today." She spooned grape jelly onto her plate.

"Why should we take a step backward? The ice is broken and it should stay that way," Heath mumbled, with his mouth already full. He closed his eyes. "Delicious."

"Thank you." Olivia accepted the compliment.

"What a great start to a dreary morning."

They both looked toward the windows where lumpy clouds hung low in a gray sky. The icy front moving across Texas seemed to be suspended over Waco.

"It's nice to offer something homemade or hot for breakfast on days like this. Tomorrow it'll be oatmeal or grits, and then scrambled eggs. We only do cold cereal and fruit on Sundays when we have fewer clients."

"Because everybody's at church, right?" He cut mocking eyes toward Olivia.

"Actually, that's true, just not for the reason

you mean." She offered a smile instead of the censure he probably expected. "A few local churches serve a hot meal to the homeless on Sundays so it's likely they go as much for the pancakes as for the praise."

"Bait, huh?"

"Whatever it takes," Olivia admitted. "Somebody's gotta get the catch near the boat and then it's up to the Lord to fill the nets."

"Mornin', Miss Livvy." Amos had materialized beside them. "I'll be ready to go as soon as these dishes are all washed and put away."

"Thanks, but—"

He whipped a red bandanna from his hip pocket just in time to catch a rumbling cough.

Olivia stood and placed a hand on his bony back as the man she'd grown to love caught his breath.

"Thanks, but I've already drafted Heath to make the pickup rounds with me today," Olivia explained to Amos. "And it sounds like you need to stay indoors anyway. I'd consider it a huge favor if you'd take charge of laundry. You're the one person I can trust not to overload the machines."

"Is laundry my punishment for getting up late this morning?" Smudges of fatigue drooped beneath his eyes.

Olivia gave him a brief squeeze. "Don't be

silly. Sleeping till six hardly makes you a lay-about. I think being out of the cold and taking it easier today would do you good. Pull a chair beside the dryers where it's warm and read the novel that's been gathering dust on your night-stand for months."

He cast a wary look toward Heath. "But it's *my* job to go along and handle the heavy stuff."

"Let's take advantage of somebody else while we have the chance. In no time Heath will be back in Austin and you'll be my main man, like always."

A small grin flipped Amos's pout upside down. He'd lived the last ten of his sixty-plus years feeling like an outcast, unworthy of love. Olivia's heart hurt for the doubt in his tired eyes. She prayed she'd never become accustomed or hardened to the fearful gaze that was common among the homeless.

"Okay, if you're sure you can manage without me," he said, seeming to accept her decision. "I admit there's an odd sorta pleasure to folding a crease into warm sheets."

"That's my guy," she encouraged Amos. She took her seat again but noted how slowly he shuffled out of the dining room. Velma needed to make sure he didn't skip lunch.

"So what's all this about heavy pickups?" Heath was on his feet, a damp cloth in his hand as he wiped crumbs from the table. Cleanliness was next to godliness. Olivia would take that as a positive sign.

"Once a week we make the rounds of local businesses to get their donations. Since I also spend time at each site networking for client jobs, it takes the better part of a day. It'll be eye-opening for you to ride along."

A frown wrinkled Heath's forehead for a moment but quickly smoothed out of sight. Was he *annoyed?*

"You got something better to do?" She quirked a brow, waited for his answer.

Will it be so bad spending the day riding around town with me? I'm no socialite, but I'm not exactly frumpy. Olivia glanced down at the plaid flannel shirt and jeans that had come out of donation bags. Better revisit that *not exactly frumpy* business.

Heath watched Olivia's gaze drift downward to her clothing. The red and black of the faded shirt against her complexion was perfect. Actually, perfect was an understatement. She didn't need fancy clothes to hide flaws. He'd noted earlier how she filled out the jeans with a woman's body, tall and proud.

Even so, a sad shadow passed over her face. Was it self-doubt? No way! Man, she was impossible to read.

"No, I don't have anything else on my calendar," he answered her question. With the staff on site there wouldn't be any chance to poke around anyway. Might as well see what more he could find out from Olivia, maybe even get some insight from the people who supported her place.

"And now that I've had a moment to think it over, there's nothing I'd rather do than learn about the mission business today." He tried to sound agreeable.

She smiled, and then looked down to collect her plate and napkin. How easy it was to please her with a lie. His skin crawled at the observation.

"Okay, then. It'll take me about thirty minutes to get the residents lined out for the day and then I'll meet you out back by the truck." Before he could reach for it, she'd grabbed her plate and headed for the kitchen.

There was an odd feeling in the pit of Heath's stomach and it wasn't just because he'd like to have another one of those buttered biscuits. He hadn't been outside in broad daylight without a cover while on a case in…actually, he'd *never* worked in the open without some form of disguise.

What if someone recognized him? Tripped him up?

And why did it matter, anyway?

I'm done being a cop. My decision hasn't changed in the past twenty-four hours.

A flash of plaid and short black hair moved past the doorway. The breath was tight in his chest as he admitted that something had changed after all.

And it had a name.

Olivia Wyatt.

Chapter Seven

Heath scrunched deeper into the lumpy passenger seat and then pulled the hood of his jacket over his baseball cap. He tugged it close to the right side of his head.

"If you're still cold I can turn the heat higher for a while," Olivia offered. "But if you're embarrassed to be riding in my old truck, you'll just have to get over it."

So she'd noticed his effort to shield his face from vehicles at each intersection.

"Oh, it's just a nervous habit." He dismissed her accusation, then fidgeted again with his collar.

"What's got you so anxious?" She angled her head, and sent a questioning look across the cab of the ancient pickup.

"Too much caffeine this morning." He straightened in the seat, relaxed his shoulders so he looked less like a turtle with its head pulled in. He glanced at the mirror to his right and noted a black and white about to pull alongside. One of the officers seemed familiar. Heath propped his right elbow on the windowsill and blocked his face with his open palm.

She leaned forward, caught sight of the vehicle beside them. "Is that it? Are you worried about the police?"

The lady was observant, and he was doing a lousy job of acting casual. Time to get a grip.

"I guess I'm a little jumpy after my recent run-in with the law."

"Oh, good grief," Olivia huffed. "It's not like you're under house arrest, forbidden to leave the shelter. What we're doing today is part of your community service and you have nothing to worry about. Besides, I know most of the traffic officers."

Just my luck, a well-connected citizen.

The light overhead flashed green. She pressed the accelerator and the truck rattled forward into the intersection. It backfired in resistance, sputtered, trembled and then died, right there in the center lane.

The cruiser moved directly behind Olivia's vehicle, flipped on blue strobes and gave a brief blast of the siren as if the cops enjoyed drawing further attention to the broken-down old Chevy.

"So much for having nothing to worry about." Heath sank back into the folds of his jacket.

"Oh, cut it out. This happens all the time," she chided.

"That would have been useful information before we left the shelter."

Olivia glanced in her rearview mirror at the approaching officer, then began cranking down her window. "All right! It's Freddy Weatherford. We went to high school together."

"Of course you did," Heath mumbled.

"Hey, gorgeous!" The cop removed his cap and poked his head in Olivia's window. "Everything okay?" He looked Heath's way, the true meaning of the question clear.

"It's all good, Freddy. I just need a push."

"Since I'm freezing and we're in the middle of an intersection you can introduce me to your friend another time." He cast Heath a glare of both interest and warning before settling the uniform cap back on his head.

Officer Weatherford stepped away from the cab and signaled his partner behind the wheel of the patrol car. The driver matched his nudge bar to the Chevy's rear bumper and accelerated gently. Olivia popped the clutch and the truck sputtered back to life. She waved appreciation and then quickly closed the window against a burst of frigid air that nearly blew off her ratty old stocking cap.

"And that happens all the time?" Heath released the breath he'd been holding.

"Since the very first day Big Red was donated. But all it takes is a push to get her started again and that's turned out to be a nice way to meet people."

"Maybe so, unless you're meeting those people late at night on the end of that dark street where you built your place."

"If you're trying to scare me out of the warehouse district you need to take a number. I've been hearing that argument since the day the Realtor showed me the property. God led me to the area of town with the most need and found me the perfect building."

He held his palms outward. "Hey, I'm just sayin'."

"Yeah, well, say it to our clients who'll be desperate to find a warm place to sleep tonight."

She swung the creaky red dinosaur into a parking space in front of a multistory brick building on Franklin Avenue.

"There are at least a dozen companies inside that I can count on for donations and job leads." She slid to the pavement, locked and slammed the door and pulled her ugly cap tight. Heath hurried to keep up. As she headed for the lobby entrance he admired the fearless tilt of her head and the confident strength of her carriage. Olivia wasn't a woman who cowered with something to hide or slept with one eye open. Her conscience seemed clear, her motives pure.

He lengthened his stride, reached for the door and swept it wide for her to enter first.

"Lead the way, boss lady."

Her chin dipped, her eyes cast toward the floor, her cheeks colored with humility.

It was no wonder her supporters were loyal.

But if Olivia Wyatt was Mother Teresa's understudy, who was running drugs through her place?

Olivia hadn't been around many technogeeks in her life, so it was taking her a while to figure Heath out. He was a lot of help once he finally loosened up, but did he ever have a suspicious nature. No wonder his parents' efforts to give him a Christian upbringing had been such a struggle. The guy wouldn't accept anything on say-so, much less faith.

It was a fruitful day. The truck bed was full of boxes that included seasonal foods as well as badly needed staples. With their Thanksgiving feast only days away, it was a relief to store up cans of yams, cranberry jelly and pumpkin pie filling.

"So, what did you think?" she asked during their ride back to the shelter.

"I think I owe you an apology."

She glanced his way to see if Heath was poking fun at her but no smile creased his face. In fact, his eyes were round, his stare intense.

"Apology for what?" she asked.

"For insinuating that you were wasting your future running a homeless shelter." Heath sat tall with his arms crossed, no longer hiding in the corner of the cab as he had earlier. "If the effort I witnessed today is a glimpse of how you operate your business, you'd get my vote for city manager if you ever decided to enter politics."

Olivia's cheeks warmed as she returned her attention to the afternoon traffic. "Apology accepted, but there's a strategic error in your thinking."

"You'd never run?"

"You can't vote in this city."

"Ah, good point." He nodded. "But seriously, Olivia, you're a passionate spokesperson and a gifted networker. You could just as easily be a marketing director with a six-figure salary."

She shook her head at the suggestion. "I wouldn't want a job like that, no matter what it paid. Working for somebody else has never appealed to me."

"Sounds like you were born to be an entrepreneur."

"I guess so. But I don't exactly think of myself that way, either."

The old bench seat creaked as he shifted to stare at her. She kept her eyes on the road.

"Then how do you see your life's work? I mean, if your personal circumstances were different, do you think you'd still be on the same career path?"

"I hope my desire to serve would be just as strong as it is today. But if my path had been different I'd probably have followed my creative passion and developed my painting. I'd be a starving but fulfilled artist."

"Really?"

The disbelief in his voice drew her glance to his face.

"Why do you find that so surprising?" Obviously, she'd read too much into his compliments for her work the night before.

"It just amazes me that given unlimited choices, you'd still be happy in a career without any guarantees."

"Nothing in life comes with guarantees, Heath. You should know that by now. Wealth doesn't buy you time or peace, and I have the family history to prove it. You can't put a price on health or integrity. I feel blessed to have those things and anything more would just be overflow."

"Points well taken," he conceded. "So, what are you doing to develop your talent?"

"I have a few canvases upstairs that I work on when there's time. Other than that, not much."

"You could be the next Grandma Moses if you'd put half the energy into your art that you put into your pitch for donations."

She snickered at his observation.

"I'm serious. You were so sharp those people never felt the blade."

"Is that your way of saying I'm sticking it to my contacts?" she teased.

"Basically, but for a good cause so it's not a bad thing. And if you ever do decide to go in another direction, you have a toolbox full of sales skills."

Glad for a reason not to look into Heath's eyes, Olivia watched her mirrors as she expertly backed Big Red up to the side entrance. She enjoyed a compliment as much as the next woman, she just wasn't sure her sales skills were what she most wanted to be admired for.

"Here we are." She set the hand brake and wrapped her woolen scarf tight before reaching for the door handle.

"Olivia?"

She swung her gaze toward the sound of his soft voice as he continued.

"All joking aside, the effort you're making for others is extraordinary. My mama used to talk about the importance of being a quiet witness. Watching you today, I finally understand what that means."

Her heart thumped as she realized he hadn't missed her occasional mention of a passage of Scripture or her offering of seasonal blessings. Maybe this man who appeared so dry was actually a dry sponge just waiting to soak up some Truth.

"Thank you, Heath. My testimony is the most important thing God packed in my toolbox."

"Miss Livvy!" Velma called from the open door. Her eyes were so wide with worry that the whites shone all around her dark irises.

"What's wrong?" Olivia's sneakers hit the pavement, slamming her door as Heath did the same.

"It's Amos. He's sicker than a dog."

"Could it be something he ate?" Olivia's insides quivered at the thought. Food-borne bacteria could spread through a shelter like wildfire, making it necessary to throw out the good along with the suspicious.

"Don't think so. He took to his bunk with a chill straight after lunch and right now he's burnin' up with fever and sounds like he might cough up a lung."

Olivia looked at Heath who gave a grim nod.

"Flu," they chorused.

"Go." He shooed her. "I'll get this stuff unloaded."

Olivia hurried to the men's dorm. Amos was curled on his side beneath several blankets. The warmth from a small space heater had the window sweating next to his bunk, yet Amos's teeth still chattered uncontrollably. Olivia remembered her own chill and raw throat from the evening before, but that seemed to have passed. She bent closer, placed the back of her fingers against his unshaved cheek.

"His temp has to be well over a hundred."

"The poor old fella's hotter than a $2 pistol," Velma agreed.

"Is anybody else showing the same symptoms?"

"Not that I know of." She shook her head.

Olivia fished in her pocket, and pulled out the key to her apartment. "Go set up the sofa bed in my living room. We'll move him upstairs just in case he's contagious."

"It's closin' the gate after the cows are out, but worth a try."

Olivia followed behind Velma. When she turned into the stairwell, Olivia continued out the exit.

Heath hefted a box filled with canned goods, handed it to Nick who headed inside and then reached for another carton. "How is he?" Heath asked.

"Velma didn't exaggerate. I'll get him moved up to my place so we can keep him quarantined."

"You get a flu shot?" He barked as if he knew what her answer might be.

She shook her head, ashamed of being short-sighted, especially in the midst of so much hype about this year's flu season.

"I meant to have somebody over from the free clinic but that detail never made it to the top of my to-do list."

"I can look after the old guy."

"You?" She couldn't help smiling at the grudging offer. She'd lay odds Heath had never filled the role of caregiver. This would be a rough initiation.

"Hey, I know I wouldn't be anybody's first choice, but I did have the good sense to take a flu shot so I'm less likely to get sick."

She gave an emphatic shake of her head. "No, my staff is my responsibility."

"Maybe so, but if you come down with the crud, who's gonna run this place?"

"Good point," Olivia agreed, knowing she was in no position to decline his offer.

When Nick returned, she asked him to finish

up the unloading. Then she motioned for Heath to follow.

"I'm pretty sure we'll have to carry him up the steps. Want me to get Bruce to help us?"

Heath cut a glance her way, an insulted squint to his eyes. "I beg your pardon, but I do occasionally get away from the computer and into the gym. I'm pretty sure I can manage his scrawny hide by myself."

"Sorry," she murmured as they passed the men's locker room, and then hurried through the bunks to Amos's bed. She'd been right, he was in no shape to walk, much less climb a flight of steps.

Heath didn't hesitate once he reached the bedside. He tossed off two blankets, tucked the third neatly around Amos's limp body and scooped the man up as effortlessly as he might lift a child.

"Lead the way," he instructed.

She moved through the familiar hallways, her handiwork on the walls a blur as a dozen questions sprang to mind. What if somebody else came down with it? Maybe she should close for a few days rather than risk making her clients sick, but where else would they go in this bitter-cold weather?

At the top of the stairs, the door to the apartment stood open. The sofa was pulled out with fresh sheets smoothed over the mattress. Heath settled Amos carefully and Olivia tucked warm blankets around his shivering body. Heath was silent. He'd stepped back and shifted his gaze to her walls. She noticed his wide-eyed stare at the unframed canvases that crowded every lateral surface of her minimal living quarters.

"We've gotta get his fever down," Olivia insisted, drawing Heath's attention back to Amos.

"I gave him aspirin a couple of hours ago but it didn't help much," Velma offered.

"Got any ibuprofen?" Heath asked. Olivia nodded and headed for her bathroom cabinet. She returned with two tablets, they propped Amos up and he swallowed the meds and a sip of water without resistance. But seconds later he burst into a fit of coughing, his chest heaving with the effort.

"Get some towels and a bucket in case he gets sick. I can handle fever and coughing but barfing is another issue altogether." Heath looked from Olivia to Velma and back to Olivia again, sweeping his hands in a hurry-up motion. "Well, give me what I asked for and then get out of here."

Olivia wasn't at all certain it was right to dump this on Heath. Community service meant he should cook and clean, not get exposed to the worst kind of seasonal sickness.

"Are you sure you want to do this, Heath?"

"Keep bugging me and I might change my mind."

"Here ya go." Velma plopped the requested items on the floor near the sofa. "Come on, Miss Livvy. Let's get away from this flu bug."

Worry settled over Olivia's heart as she moved slowly toward her door. It was late, there were clients to check in for the night and dinner to serve. She had no idea what kind of shape the kitchen was in and if Amos had been sick all day that probably meant the laundry was stacked up.

"You comin', Miss Livvy? There's a bunk open next to me, I'll make it up for you after dinner."

She had no choice but to leave the two men alone in her apartment, her private sanctuary. It wasn't like there was anything of value in the place, but these few small rooms were her home. She glanced around at the meager, secondhand furnishings and many original paintings, then followed Velma into the stairwell and closed the door from the outside.

This wasn't even close to how Heath had planned to get into Olivia's apartment, but it would work. He looked down at the thin form of the man passed out on the sofa bed.

As long as he could keep Amos medicated

and asleep, he'd be free to search to his heart's content, Heath thought to himself.

But at the mention of his heart, it seemed to ache a bit. He was going to invade the lady's private space. And, as he'd just discovered, it seemed to be hung wall-to-wall with incredible art that he'd wager had never seen the light of day. Her talent deserved to be celebrated, not locked away inside a shelter that was under surveillance by the police. He felt another twinge of guilt. Well, he'd just have to get over this dose of conscience, and in a hurry. There was no room for regret in undercover work.

Heath was about to tiptoe toward Olivia's bedroom when Amos struggled to support himself on one elbow like he was determined to share some news.

He opened his mouth to speak. Instead, he began to heave.

Chapter Eight

Two changes of bedsheets later and Heath was afraid he might be sick himself.

But the last three hours of tending to a sick person had taught Heath a new sense of respect for his mama. The woman had a constitution of steel. Not much had bothered her when Heath was growing up. She hadn't shuddered when he'd come home with a nail through his hand, hadn't shrieked when he'd wrestled a wounded squirrel from the cat next door, and never shied away when too much partying left a fraternity brother in a disgusting heap on her bathroom floor.

Now that Heath thought about it, she'd never even hounded him on those occasions. Not unless he counted her scriptural references on each subject as hounding, and back then he had. While he scrubbed his hands for the umpteenth time he made a mental note to send his mama flowers and a thank-you card.

"Heath?" Olivia called, her voice loud over knuckles hammering at the locked door.

He hurried to answer before she disturbed Amos, who'd only just settled back down. Heath cracked the door a few inches expecting a dinner delivery that wouldn't appeal to him no matter what was on the plate.

Olivia's face was flushed, pink and gleaming from warmth. Her eyes were wide, almost panicky.

"What's wrong?" He pulled the door wider but didn't want her to come closer for fear of Amos's nasty germs.

"Bruce just passed out in the men's room."

"Not another one," Heath muttered, knowing the answer. A runaway train was bearing down on him and there was no way to stop it. "I suppose you want to bring him up here."

"We don't have any choice. Nick will be along in a minute with a roll-away bed and as soon as it's made up I'll need you to help us get Bruce upstairs."

Good grief! One sick guy I can handle, but with two I'm never gonna get this apartment searched.

"Have you considered taking them to the emergency room? Amos has been a handful so maybe that's the best place."

Olivia shook her head, pushed past and headed for the small closet where he'd found extra sheets. "I already called two hospitals. They're swamped and won't do anything more than test to confirm the flu and then send both men back here with medical bills they can't pay."

She pulled out the remaining linens, tossed them on a chair, then pushed a footstool and table against the wall, presumably to clear a path for the cot.

"Miss Livvy?" Nick stood in the doorway they'd left open.

"Right here, Nick," she directed him.

The roll-away snapped together and fifteen minutes later Bruce was shivering beneath blankets, complaining of the worst headache of his life.

Heath motioned for Olivia to join him in her small kitchen, kept his voice low. "Are these garden-variety flu symptoms or could it be something worse?"

"I Googled this year's strain. Fever, chills, aches and cough are common. Most people don't get the stomach issues."

"Well, Amos won the flu lottery this year, because he's got it all." Heath pointed to the large shopping bag stuffed with sheets. "Better get these washed and back up to me. I have a feeling the night shift in the infirmary might be a busy one."

Olivia's spine slumped as a visible shudder passed through her body. Heath hoped it was a sign of concern and not illness. If this tough lady started sinking he'd have to find a way to call for backup. And if he did that after less than two days on the case, he'd never hear the end of it from the guys in his unit. He felt a twinge of shame for his selfish thoughts.

"I'm sorry about this, Heath. If you want to change your mind and help out downstairs, I'll trade duties with you."

"Nope." He grabbed the handles of the paper bag, turned her around and marched her as best he could toward the door. "Go take care of your business. Being up here only increases the chance you'll come down with it, too."

She pointed toward an old-fashioned black phone mounted on the wall. "If you need anything, give us a call downstairs. Just press the pound sign and it'll ring at the front desk and in the kitchen. Nothing's off-limits up here, so make yourself at home."

"Got it. Now get away from these germs."

At the door she paused. "Heath, I need to ask you for another favor. The Bible says that when two or more are gathered in God's name, He is present. Will you agree with me in prayer?" She dropped the paper bag and held both hands outward, like a child needing the comfort of touch. "Please?"

He'd watched her every move for almost twenty-four hours. Her nature was the antithesis of his. She was a giver and everything she did was out of concern for others. How could he deny her such a small request? Heath pressed his palms to hers, and tried to ignore the electricity where his fingers and Olivia's touched. She squeezed his hands, bowed her head and he did the same.

"Father God, Your mercy is new every day. You are bigger than our needs, bigger than this illness, bigger than our worries. I pray Your healing powers upon Bruce and Amos, I plead Your protection over everyone else in the shelter and I praise You for Your boundless love that no one can fathom. Thank you, Lord, for sending Heath to Table of Hope at a time when You knew I would need his help. He is a blessing and a treasure. In the sweet name of Jesus we pray. Amen."

Heath was fortunate that Olivia turned and hurried down the stairs instead of waiting for his reaction to her prayer. There was a pumpkin-size lump in his throat, and he couldn't have spoken in his own defense if a SWAT team kicked in the door.

He wasn't worthy of her kind words, but he was grateful for them. She thought his presence at Table of Hope was somehow God's doing. How hurt the sweet lady would be when she learned the truth. Olivia certainly wouldn't call Heath a *blessing* if she knew he was about to trespass on her private space, searching for clues to her guilt.

Or her innocence.

It was several hours before Amos and Bruce were asleep at the same time and Heath was free to poke around. He gently probed Olivia's personal belongings, careful to leave everything as he found it. He admired each piece of original art before checking for anything secured to its backside. Remorse over violating another person's privacy was an unfamiliar and unsettling feeling. He'd like to ignore the new emotions that had crept into his mind and stirred his heart since he'd crossed the threshold at Table of Hope. But overlooking hard facts had never been his style.

And he couldn't pretend there was nothing to be suspicious about when he spotted the old-fashioned hope chest in the back of Olivia's closet with its cedar lid fastened tight. If nothing was off-limits, as she'd said, why the need to keep something under lock and key when it was already buried out of sight?

Heath rifled through the drawers of the small kitchen and bathroom for something to pick the antique lock. He was generally a fair locksmith with a letter opener or cuticle scissors but every effort proved frustrating in this case. Too much probing would cause damage to a piece that might be a family heirloom. His search warrant didn't mention anything about being careful, but this was Olivia's private property, after all.

"What is wrong with this picture?" he grumbled. Caring about a person under suspicion created too much drama.

"Help me." Bruce's cry was weak.

Heath backed out of Olivia's closet and turned into the hallway to find the man prostrate on the floor only halfway into the bathroom.

Oh, Lord, help me, too! Heath had little time to consider whether or not his short prayer would be welcome in heaven. But he was certain his presence would be welcome in the bathroom.

He pushed up his sleeves and went to work.

Olivia stood alone in the kitchen, absentmindedly drying the last of the soup bowls while she prayed.

"Abba Father, this is the first night since we opened our doors that I haven't had someone to share worship with me. Please rest your healing hand over our staff and place a hedge of

protection around Heath. We are so grateful You sent him to us. May Your will for his life be undeniable in the hours he's at Table of Hope. Amen."

A thump and scraping noises drew her eyes toward the ceiling. She wasn't accustomed to sounds of movement overhead. Her stomach quivered each time she thought of poor Heath all alone with two very sick men to care for. But he was a healthy guy who'd been immunized against the seasonal bug, and he was so insistent.

What choice did she have anyway? Her other residents were doing all they could, but the evening had been an uphill battle. Velma made it through check-in, all the while complaining about a throbbing head and an aching back. Nick's tired eyes and constant cough caused him to miss class and crawl back into his bunk, ostensibly for a nap, but he hadn't been seen outside the men's dorm for hours.

Another muffled thump rattled the kitchen ceiling. She hoped it wasn't one of her friends collapsing on the floor of her tiny apartment. Olivia was thankful she'd found someone to spell Heath, who was bound to be worn out by now. When she'd asked for client volunteers to help with dinner, several regulars who'd had flu shots were identified. One of them was Dick Sheehan. He'd been a medic in the Army and said he didn't have any problem caring for a couple of sick guys for a while. She'd sent him upstairs to relieve Heath a few minutes earlier.

The intercom phone buzzed.

"This is Olivia," she answered.

"What do you know about this guy?" Heath's voice was muffled, as if he was covering his mouth.

"You mean Dick?"

"That's who he claims he is, anyway." His suspicious nature was raging.

"I have no reason to believe otherwise."

"You shouldn't let strangers up here in your home," Heath barked. "He could be an axe murderer for all you know."

"And so could you!" she bit back. "Look, you have to rest eventually. Dick says he has medical training, so let him help for a while."

"I hope he's trained in getting pain relievers and orange juice down a guy's gullet and then cleaning up the stuff that won't stay there."

Olivia dipped her chin and covered her eyes. Sooner or later illness was bound to hit the shelter and she just had to deal with whatever issues came along with it. Right now getting Heath to follow her instructions was the issue.

"Heath, that's all the more reason for you to get away for a little bit. Come on downstairs and have something to eat." She stood her ground.

"Ugh. My appetite went out the door with the first bag of trash."

"At least let me make you a peanut butter sandwich."

She waited for his acquiescence, wondering if his reluctance had to do with food or with leaving Dick in her apartment. Either way, Heath needed to take a break.

"Hello?" she prompted.

"I'll be down as soon as I give Sheehan instructions and I'm convinced he can handle things for a while."

She hung the receiver back on the hook and felt her lips curl into a smile. His servant's heart was emerging and he was being the hands of Christ whether or not that was the original purpose for Heath's days at Table of Hope.

She came out of the pantry several minutes later to find his brown eyes glaring at her from the kitchen doorway.

"Perfect timing! I'm finished in the kitchen and ready to start Bible study." Olivia bit the inside of her lip to hold back laughter at the way his jaw sagged in disbelief.

"What do you mean Bible study?"

"You know exactly what I mean. As soon as dinner is cleared away we always meet in the big room for worship and study."

"Even with the sick folks we have upstairs, and all the work we need to do down here?"

Olivia's heart danced against her ribs at Heath's use of *we,* as if he felt like part of the staff.

"This place is in crisis," he insisted.

"And that's why we need to take a moment to ground ourselves in God's grace and mercy. All good things come from Him and He's our rock in times of trouble."

Heath closed his eyes, gave his head a slight shake of disbelief and then fixed his gaze on her again.

"I get it, Olivia. Faith is a big deal to you and I admire that. But sometimes we have to adjust for reality." He swept his palm outward to indicate his surroundings. "You can't require people to crowd into a room that might be filled with germs."

"The only ones required to participate are you and me and both of us have already been exposed to the flu."

"What about your front desk girl and that kid at the back door?"

"I've sent them both to bed. If they're not better in the morning, we'll move Nick upstairs with you and I'll call a local church about finding a volunteer to take Velma in for a few days."

Heath released a loud sigh. "Sounds like you've got it all figured out."

"No, I don't, but God does." She dropped her apron into the laundry hamper and squeezed a clear blob of hand sanitizer on her palm. "Now, grab that covered dish with your soup and sandwich and let's go see what His Word has to say about the Fruit of the Spirit."

He picked up the tray, sniffed at the soup beneath the cover and nodded approval. "I think you're right, I do need to eat. Maybe it will improve my disposition."

Heath caught her smiling behind her hand.

"Go ahead. Laugh. I know I'm a grouch. I admit that I didn't possess much of that spiritual fruit when I got here yesterday and what little I had is long gone."

"And that's why Jesus said, 'My grace is sufficient for you, for My power is made perfect in weakness.'"

"Since you're gonna quote Scripture at me anyway we might as well go to the big room and get comfortable. I'll need a strong cup of coffee to help me swallow another dose of religion." His comment wasn't exactly music to her ears but at least he was cooperating.

What more could a girl want from a man who was practically sweeping her off her feet?

Chapter Nine

During his years undercover, Heath had spent many a night in discomfort.

Like the time he lay for hours in a ditch, still as death beneath a pile of leaves. An unexpected drug purchase went down a few feet from his face, but he couldn't blow his cover and raise his head. The only parts of the dealers he could identify were their lousy shoes!

More aggravating was the costume party where he was staked out in a Spider-Man outfit, mistaken for some reveler's college friend and forced to do the hokey pokey to avoid exposure. When you have two left feet, *that's* what it's all about!

Even so, Heath couldn't recall a night more uncomfortable than the one spent in Olivia's apartment. Nick's fever shot up at midnight so he packed a small bag and moved upstairs to sleep on another roll-away. Every forty-five minutes Heath attended to one man or the other, and in between he groped about Olivia's small home as quietly as possible.

Rummaging through her personal things made his conscience ache in a way he hadn't known possible. It was akin to rifling through a woman's handbag, something his mom had once said was the ultimate invasion of privacy. As he explored each nook where drugs might be stashed he found himself repeating the final passage from the night's teaching.

The Lord detests lying lips, but He delights in men who are truthful.

Heath basically lied for a living, so that Proverb rolled over him like water off a duck's back. But it grieved him to think Olivia's integrity could possibly be for show, either a cover for herself or the father who'd abandoned her. Women had that weird thing about wanting to believe in their fathers, no matter what sort of creeps they'd been. It would be just like Olivia to forgive Dalton Wyatt, but would she compromise herself and become an accomplice in his crimes?

Heath doubted that either of his sisters lost much sleep worrying about redeeming their murdering old man. Part of what he'd told Olivia about losing his parents had been true. He just hadn't proffered the important detail that his mother had died at the hands of his raging father, an act of violence that turned three kids—not just one—into orphans. Heath's adoptive parents must have thought he carried a bad seed that they needed to smother with faith. From his earliest memories they'd involved him in church activities, but it never felt natural to him as it did with Olivia.

His insides churned and squirmed. The discomfort had little to do with the three sick stomachs in the apartment and everything to do with his night of searching for clues. Each time he came up empty-handed he breathed a sigh of relief, blotting out the idea that Olivia could be implicated, much less guilty.

Heath felt something special for her. If he knew what love was like, he might even say he loved her. But it was too soon for that, wasn't it?

He struggled to force the thoughts from his mind and concentrate on the job. Then, just before dawn, Heath hit the jackpot.

Returning to the bathroom closet where Olivia stacked sheets and towels, his fingertips grazed a lump of plastic he was certain hadn't been there earlier. Reaching deeper he grasped the article, whispered "Come to Papa," and pulled it from behind the recently laundered items. The quart-size, heat-sealed bag contained hundreds of green tablets Heath recognized as Ecstasy. The junk had been a club favorite since the eighties. Thankfully, it had taken a dip in popularity, but in recent months it was back with a vengeance and more dangerous than before, since it was often laced with very addictive meth.

As he stared at the poison in the bag, his heart thumped out the answer. *Dick Sheehan.* He had to be the source of this stash.

"Oh, use your head. It can't be that easy." Heath cautioned himself against a rush to judgment. He was looking to find guilt apart from Olivia and he knew it. The truth was that she'd personally handled the laundry and had been the one to restock the linen closet.

Still, Sheehan had been quick to offer help that gained him entry to Olivia's place for several hours.

It was time to pay a visit to Biddle and check out some mug shots. It would be easy enough to get fingerprints of everybody who'd had access while Amos, Bruce and Nick were passed out. Or Heath could simply lift prints off the sides of the porcelain commode while nobody was hugging it. Might as well run each man through the computer as long as he was going to the station. That would help cut this job short before Heath got any more exposure to sick folks.

Or went any further down the dangerous, dead-end road that seemed to be leading to a head-on collision between his heart and Olivia Wyatt's.

Olivia stacked bowls in the cabinet and then ran her towel over the counter to soak up any last drops of dishwater. She'd hated offering cold cereal on a freezing morning, but with her staff dropping like mercury in the thermometer outside, it was the best she could do. If it came down to it, their clients could eat corn flakes and sandwiches until the flu ran its course. At least folks would be fed, if not well fed.

"Good morning." Heath stepped inside the kitchen, causing her weary pulse to race. Bundled up beneath several layers of clothing, he headed straight for the coffee station. He dropped his backpack on the counter and reached into the storage shelf for the small stash of to-go cups.

"Everybody's finally asleep at the same time upstairs. You think Sheehan would cover for me again for a few hours?"

"I'm sure he would." She didn't dare mention Heath's change of heart over Dick's trustworthiness. "At breakfast he offered to stick around all day and help since we're shorthanded. You seem to be headed somewhere." Olivia tried to sound casual when she was anything but calm. The last thing she needed was to have Heath bail out on her.

She was shaky from lack of sleep, worried sick about the condition of her residents and worn out from running breakfast service alone. She was close to the breaking point, something she hadn't felt since her father took off.

"I gotta go get some fresh air and pick up some stuff at a drugstore." He kept his hood pulled forward, his face hidden from her view. He was intentionally avoiding eye contact. Was it really possible that he planned to walk out the door and never come back? Maybe he was going over to the police station to tell Detective Biddle that county lockup was preferable to the conditions at Table of Hope.

"Heath, nobody would blame you if you looked into other community service options."

His chin popped up, and the dark hood shrouding his face fell away as he impaled her with eyes that seemed offended.

"Is that what you think of me? That I'd take off and leave you to deal with this mess by yourself?"

The fatigue that Olivia had been fighting back finally spilled past her resolve. She pressed the damp towel to her eyes with both hands and gave herself over to a sob.

"Hey! Don't do that," Heath said with a comforting tone.

His footsteps thumped across the linoleum.

He was so close she could hear the rustle of his clothing. Surprise shuddered through Olivia's body when strong arms settled cautiously around her shoulders and folded her to his chest.

She pressed her face against him, dish towel and all, and let the worries flow out with a brief burst of rare tears. He patted her back rather awkwardly, as if he'd seen the kind gesture but never done it himself. Even in her misery Olivia had to wonder if his effort was just perfunctory, a male reaction to an emotional female, or if he was fumbling his way through a first-time experience.

Heath seemed to be sincere in his effort to offer comfort but Olivia recognized that he wasn't quite sure how to go about it. Was there a grown man without a selfish agenda as far as women were concerned in this world?

Gently with both hands, she pushed away from Heath's self-conscious embrace. Olivia dabbed at her eyes with the towel and passed her fingers through a mop of hair that hadn't been professionally styled for months. She inhaled deeply, filled her lungs.

"Don't apologize." He was quick to speak first. "If I had your stress on my shoulders and everybody around me was being KO'd, I'd be howling like a scalded dog. My mama always said a few tears could wash away a world of stress."

"I wish it was that simple. It's not so much stress as it is déjà vu."

"Wanna talk about it?" he asked, though she sensed he was anxious to be on his way.

"You have time to listen?" Her voice was embarrassingly hopeful.

"Even if you count every bit of the last two days I still have fifty-two hours on my sentence. Is that enough time for you?"

"With the way things are going around here you probably wish you could spend the rest of those hours in solitary confinement."

He unzipped his jacket, slipped off the black knit cap that covered his nearly shaved head and leaned against the kitchen countertop. "I'm here for the duration. What's happened to make you think otherwise?"

"It actually happened years ago when my dad left me to fend for myself. When the most important man in a girl's life abandons her, she can't help but expect the same treatment over and over again."

"And has that been your experience?"

"It's been my general observation. Choosing social work for my education and managing a shelter has exposed me to more abandoned people than I can count. I'm not so discouraged that I don't have hope, but right now I only trust in one relationship. People will lie to your face but God is not a man that He should lie."

"Don't you think there are times when shooting straight is the wrong way to go?" Heath's eyes darkened, his face tensed. "If everybody went around saying whatever they thought, you can just imagine how many people would get hurt."

"That's a rationalization if I ever heard one." She tossed the towel and her apron into the laundry hamper. "If my father had looked me in the eye, told me he'd made terrible mistakes and that he was running away, that would have been a lot less painful than letting me learn about his lies for myself."

"No man wants to admit his failings, least of all to his own kid."

"But I might still respect him if he had. Instead he made up some story about a business trip so I wouldn't be suspicious of his packing. He failed to mention he never intended to come back."

"So he just took off?" Heath's voice was incredulous.

"Yep." All these years later she couldn't believe it, either. "But he owed a lot of money to the IRS so the Feds were pretty hot on his heels. He'd only been gone a few days when a couple of guys in dark suits came to the door. I guarantee that's no way to find out you've been sucker punched."

Heath held his palm open toward her as he nodded agreement. Olivia hesitantly slipped her hand into his, almost reluctant to accept his overture.

"Men are selfish creatures." His voice was soft. He tugged her fingers for emphasis. "Some of the things we do seem to make perfectly good sense to us in the beginning but then turn out disastrous in the end."

She stared into his eyes. "Is that wisdom from personal experience?"

"Mostly, as you just said, it's been my general observation."

"Your time here is going a long way toward changing my perspective." She gave a light squeeze to the hand still holding hers. "God always has a plan if we only give Him time to work it out."

Heath let his hand fall to his side, turned back to the coffeepot and busied himself dumping sugar into a paper cup.

"Well, I can't speak for God's plan, but if mine works out I'll be back around lunchtime." He snapped on a plastic lid, then pulled his cap over his dusting of dark hair and zipped his jacket. "I'd like to think they're past the stomach flu upstairs but the fever and coughing need attention. So after I take care of some personal business, I'll pick up more supplies from the drugstore."

"You know the forecast is for freezing rain, don't you?"

Heath's face was handsomely in need of a shave as he scrunched his brows and lips into a grimace. "Hopefully it won't materialize. That always slows down the city buses."

"Take the Chevy."

"You don't mind?"

"As long as you don't mind being seen in it." She grinned. "Let me grab the cash box and I'll give you some money for the pharmacy."

He frowned, refusing the offer. "I've got it."

"Thanks, Heath." She'd learned early in life to accept charity with grace. It served her well in running the shelter. "Other than sending Dick up there to keep an eye on things, is there anything else you need?"

"Yeah." He took a step toward her, his long arms twitched at the sides of his body as if he was unsure what to do with them.

"Yeah, there's something I need, Olivia." She sensed he was about to hug her, but then he seemed to give up, fisted both hands and stepped back.

"Just name it."

"Prayer."

"For the guys upstairs?"

"For me." Heath swept his hood over his head, jangled her keys, grabbed his backpack and left without explaining his request.

Chapter Ten

Heath flopped down in the chair, leaned forward to rest his elbows on Biddle's desk and slanted an accusing look at his mentor.

"Did you know Olivia Wyatt is a card carryin' Christian?"

"Was the Scripture over the front entrance your first clue or did you find out the hard way by putting your big foot in your mouth?"

"I haven't blown anything if that's what you're asking, but some warning might have been helpful. And life would be easier if you had let me go in disguise."

Biddle snorted, buffed a palm across his gray crew cut as if rubbing away a headache. "I don't recall any promise from the department to make your life easier when you were sworn in, but there was somethin' in the oath about you faithfully obeying orders."

"And I am, but I kinda feel exposed. This is like goin' into a firefight without a weapon."

"David stood up to Goliath with just a sling-shot and a stone."

Heath slumped back in the chair. "You, too?" he muttered. "I can't swing a cat these days with-out hittin' a Christian."

Biddle nodded. "It doesn't say much for my witness that you've worked with me for years and didn't know I was a believer."

"Hey, it's not like we got a class in officer training on spotting the signs. But if I had to guess, I'd peg you as a churchgoer."

"What about you, Heath?"

"Hey, I didn't drive all the way over here in that rattletrap to talk about Sunday school. It's colder than a well digger's behind in that old truck!"

"Why didn't you call for a pickup? I could have sent an unmarked."

"Just because the car's unmarked doesn't mean I'm not. Climbing in the backseat could put a bull's eye on my chest."

Biddle leaned closer, folded his thick arms and rested them on a mess of paperwork. "You sayin' we got a snitch in the ranks?" His voice was low.

"Anything's possible and you know it, but that's not what I meant." As he mirrored Biddle's guarded position, Heath recalled the face of the traffic officer who'd given him the once-over. "Olivia seems to be well-connected with the black-and-whites, thanks to that clunker she drives. Yesterday an officer named Weatherford gave her a push out of an intersection. I was in the cab and got the evil eye from the guy."

"Don't know him." Biddle shook his head. "You afraid of being recognized?"

"Only if it ties undercover activity to Olivia. You know how fast gossip travels in this town, whether it's true or not."

"Is that because you think she's in the clear?"

"I'd swear on my life she has no idea where her old man's hiding out or that there's activity running through her place," Heath insisted. "In fact, she's one of the most straight up and giving people I've ever met. She's on a mission from God, so to speak, and I don't want to see that spoiled. Any connection to this operation will be bad news for the folks who depend on her."

"Sounds like you're getting personally invested over there. Pretty quick, isn't it?"

Heath straightened in his chair, squared his shoulders and gave Biddle a pointed look. "I'm just doin' my job."

Biddle stared hard, as if he could see into

Heath's soul. "You always have, but I don't recall this compassionate streak in you before."

"Well, maybe it's like the flu. Highly contagious."

"Or maybe it was there all along."

Their gazes locked for one, two, three seconds. Then both men spewed laughter and fell back against their chairs.

"Nah, I don't think so, either," Biddle agreed, rolling his eyes in a gimme-a-break fashion. "Let's get those prints to the lab and see what the computer tells us."

Heath stood to follow Biddle from the office. "We gotta figure out who's driving this bus so we can steer it away from Table of Hope and run it into a ditch someplace else."

"And then what?"

Heath hitched a shoulder—no idea. But he knew what Olivia would suggest, so he went straight to her Source.

Biddle just asked a good question, God. When this is done, then what? And it would sure be nice if You'd answer pretty quick.

Heath slung his backpack and a Walgreens shopping bag over his shoulder and rang Table of Hope's front bell. An unfamiliar woman with big hair pressed the door release and waved him inside.

"I'm Heath Stone," he said to the middle-aged lady behind the check-in counter.

"Nice to meet cha, Heath. Name's Mary Sue Stratton. Miss Livvy told me to expect you eventually." Mary Sue spoke and popped her gum simultaneously. "I'm coverin' for Velma."

"So she's no better today?"

"Not from what I hear. Miss Livvy called Grace Chapel and they sent somebody over to pick Velma up and look after her for a few days. This old world wouldn't survive a week if it wasn't for the willingness of a servant's heart."

A servant's heart.

What a way to explain it. That's exactly what beat in Olivia's chest. In only a few days he'd come to admire her so much. Her peaceful glow attracted others like June bugs to a porch light. And this morning her tears made her even more appealing, as she'd given him a glimpse at her unguarded state.

After what her stinkin' father had put her through, she was right not to take anybody at face value. But here she was blindly putting her trust in an undercover cop who'd concocted a sad story. The really sad part is he had evidence that could be used against her if he couldn't prove her innocence.

God, You need to protect Olivia from liars.

Like me.

The buzzer hummed again. Mary Sue turned her attention to the newcomer and Heath escaped the draft of the door by heading for the kitchen. As he passed through the wide hallway he slowed to admire the incredible murals Olivia had created. He considered the canvases upstairs, seeing them as puzzle pieces waiting to be fitted together on a grand scale. The world beyond this concrete block building should know what a unique talent Olivia possessed, and today he'd ignited what he hoped would be a chain reaction.

"You need help?" Heath asked as he stepped across the threshold into the kitchen that still smelled of last night's delicious soup.

Olivia's head snapped up from the work of slicing hoagie loaves on the cutting board.

"Hey, you're back." Relief flooded the clear skin of her face, relaxing the lines of stress around her eyes. Heath's pulse thudded. Was her reaction just because he represented an extra pair of hands? Or was it because the extra pair of hands belonged to him?

"Everything go okay with the truck?" she asked.

"No problems with the relic today."

He shifted his shopping bags to set his backpack on the counter.

"We're doing cold cuts and what's left of last night's soup so I've got it covered in here. I'm sure the guys upstairs will be glad to see you. Dick couldn't stick around after all."

"What?" Heath wanted to throttle the guy. "Sheehan never went up, not even to check on them?" It would be unconscionable to leave people who were so sick to fend for themselves.

"Hold on," she calmly insisted. "He was upstairs for a little while but then he had to leave. That's when I went up to take some juice and toast, but there wasn't much interest."

"You shouldn't keep exposing yourself to that germfest," Heath insisted.

"How else am I supposed to look after sick people when I'm left by myself? Call out the National Guard?"

He deserved the sarcasm after abandoning her all morning. Instead of waiting for the questions that would require new lies he raised the Walgreens sacks to change the subject.

"You're right. Sorry I took so long, but I'm here now. Better get these things upstairs and see how everybody's doing. The lady at the front desk said Velma's not any better."

Olivia's mouth twisted as if she'd had a nasty thought. "The symptoms started early and I knew I had to get her out of the shelter. Bless her heart, she was almost too sick to walk to the car." Olivia raised her eyes again. "Heath, if one more person comes down with this I'm gonna have to take it as a sign we need to close up shop for a few days. I hate to send my clients further away in this cold but I can't risk making them all sick."

"I have to agree. The fewer people who get around this stuff, the better." And it would give him time to dig deeper into what little information he had without a constant stream of transients in and out of the place.

Besides, Olivia could use a break before she had a meltdown.

"Since I'm not showing any symptoms, I thought I'd volunteer at another shelter to offset the extra work caused by our clients."

"You are certifiably crazy!" The accusation rushed out of Heath's mouth. From the expression on her face the comment struck Olivia like a slap. But good grief, she needed to rest and unpack those bags beneath her eyes instead of chasing after more responsibility.

"Honestly, Olivia, you need to let somebody else worry about the world for a while."

"If it's insane to want to help people less fortunate than myself, then lock me in a padded cell."

"I didn't mean that the way it came out." Another lie, because he had meant it. He was selfish, just like the men he'd alluded to earlier, always thinking about things from his own perspective, and that was unlikely to change. This compassion business that Biddle mentioned was overrated. Still, Heath wished he could smooth away the lines of worry he'd just put between Olivia's haunting eyes.

"Look, let the other shelter pick up the slack. You're needed right here to help me take care of your sick buddies. I can't do it without you."

"You're right." Her shoulders sagged. Her expression changed but didn't clear. It was like dark clouds giving way to dense fog as she went from one concern to another. "I guess I hadn't thought that through. There's a lot that needs to be done around here."

He was a dunce, making things worse by the minute. He needed to say something positive.

"And I'm gonna be right beside you. Let's concentrate on getting the germs out of here in time for Thanksgiving and then everybody can enjoy the holiday."

A smile touched her lips. "That sounded downright hopeful."

"I don't know what came over me. Maybe I need a nap." He was grateful that the mood had shifted.

"Did you get any sleep at all last night?"

He slipped out of his old jacket and cap and shook his head. "A few winks in the recliner, but I don't need much."

"You can sleep in my room, you know. There's

no reason to be uncomfortable in a chair when there's a bed nearby."

"I wouldn't even consider invading your privacy by going into your bedroom." Another whopper.

The creases above the bridge of her nose softened, the sparkle slipped back into Olivia's dark eyes. How little it took to please her.

"You're a gentleman, Heath Stone." The words were sincere.

"There are plenty of folks who'd disagree with your opinion."

"Well, maybe they just don't know you the way I do."

Yep, there's no doubt about it, Lord. The lady is becoming too trusting for her own good. As long as You're taking requests, how about doing something about that, too?

Chapter Eleven

As Olivia watched Heath head down the hall carrying a load of pharmacy bags, the strangest sensation shivered over her skin. Knowing he'd once again climb the steps and enter her apartment was comforting as well as disconcerting. She didn't fully understand the reason for either feeling.

Three other residents were up there already, so it wasn't as if Heath were alone in her home or couldn't be trusted. And beyond her mother's personal Bible studies, which Olivia kept locked away in the cedar chest she'd purchased at a Goodwill store, there was absolutely nothing of value in her private quarters.

Of course, there were the canvases, but they weren't important except to Olivia. Her painting never would be of value without art classes to develop her raw talent. So she used her limited ability as a means to find solace during times when her spirit was restless. It was a blessing to concentrate on something besides problems once in a while. Olivia glanced across the hall at one of the murals she'd created during those final weeks of construction. The walls had to be painted anyway, and she got some stress relief as a trade-off for her hours of work.

There was a thud at the end of the hall as the heavy security door closed. She imagined Heath would be climbing the stairs, almost to the top. As he stepped inside, would he judge the second-hand furnishings, contrasting them to his own and find them wanting?

Web guys were supposed to be well-paid. Did Heath have a fine place in the suburbs of Austin? Or maybe a bachelor's loft in a restored downtown building near the nightlife of Sixth Street? Had the skills that allowed him to hack into the city network also earned him a lifestyle that made hers look pathetic by comparison?

He'd questioned how her present choices would limit her future potential. Did Heath think she was a failure? The breath caught in her throat as she considered the answer.

"Miss Livvy," Mary Sue called from the end of the hall, interrupting her thoughts. "Erica just checked in for volunteer duty. But she's coughin' as if she might bust a gut. I felt her forehead and she's roastin' like a chicken on a spit."

Olivia lifted her eyes to the ceiling in surrender. *Forgive me and my big mouth for even mentioning a sign, Lord. I know what I have to do now.*

Two hours and a dozen phone calls later, a crisis plan had been set in motion. The good folks at My Brother's Keeper agreed to use their fifteen-passenger van to shuttle clients for a few days as long as Olivia would help with meals. She was busy rolling fat hoagie sandwiches in plastic wrap when the black wall phone jangled. She grabbed the handset, praying it wasn't more bad news.

"I'll be in there to help you as soon as I get these guys downstairs into the showers and then squared away in the men's dorm."

"I don't know what I'd have done the last few days without you, Heath." Olivia heard the quiver in her voice. It was depressing to be so exhausted when there was so much yet to do. "You must think I'm a big baby."

"Yeah, a big *tired* baby. And once I've scrubbed your place down with Lysol you can crawl into your own bed and sleep while I keep an eye on things tonight."

"You'll have some help," she was glad to say. "Dick's back and he's working the front desk right now. As soon as everybody's shuttled over to My Brother's Keeper, he says he'll be right up."

"I'll just bet he did," Heath muttered.

She opened her mouth to ask what he meant by the comment but decided it really didn't matter. As much as she wanted everybody under her roof to get along, that simply wasn't reasonable to expect. Men forced into situations not of their making generally suffered from battered egos. Add alpha characteristics and you got a mad dog looking for a fight. Even so, this was still her place.

"Heath, if Dick's willing—"

"Look, I've got the cleanup covered," he interrupted. "And once you're back into your apartment, I don't want you opening your door to anyone else, you understand?" He was emphatic, speaking to her like he had some right.

"It might shock you to hear that before this flu hit I was doing quite well for myself. I don't need to be told how to run my business." Olivia was equally adamant.

"I'm sorry, I know I'm stepping on your toes." His apologies were becoming more frequent and less sincere. "I just don't want you to risk filling your place up with germs again once we get it disinfected and aired out. Make sense?"

"Well, when you put it that way, I guess it does."

"Okay, let me off the phone so I can get these guys down one at a time. And before you go there, no I don't need Sheehan's help."

"Heath?"

"What?"

"Have you eaten today?" Olivia asked

"Not since breakfast."

"Grab an apple from my little fridge in the kitchen. Didn't your mama ever tell you low blood sugar makes you grumpy?"

"My mama told me I was grumpy in general."

"Once again, your mama was right."

The rooms smelled of sickness. Heath raised the kitchen window an inch, glad to find solid burglar bars beyond the glass. Fat lot of good it did when Olivia not only let the criminals come inside, but also fed them dinner and gave them a place to sleep!

Before he got busy with the sick guys, he double-checked the closet. The bag of "X" was definitely gone. Heath wished he'd followed through on his fantasy of putting a spring-loaded rat trap beside the stash of pills to smack that creep Sheehan's fingers! He was definitely the culprit. He'd come up that morning just long enough to retrieve his junk and then took off, probably to make a sale.

If not for this blasted flu outbreak, Heath would be in a beard and ski parka out on the street in search of his most reliable informant. He felt sure his buddy would know where those green pills ended up. It was tempting to follow through on that idea and set up some busts. There was nothing quite as rewarding as the look on a dealer's face when he turned his product and his money over to the police. *At gunpoint.*

But recreation would have to wait for another day. It was more critical to tag the source bringing the dope into Waco. Heath needed to work fast to get this mess away from Olivia and keep it that way before it ruined everything she'd built.

He folded himself into a chair at her tiny kitchen table to ponder the fact that Olivia had also been in this apartment today. Even given her unlimited access, he didn't for a moment consider the woman who was constantly on his mind to be a suspect. He shivered more from that revelation than from the freezing wind whistling beneath the windowsill.

"I'm not thinkin' like a cop anymore. It's a good thing this is my last gig and now I've got backup."

With Biddle's help on the outside Heath could afford to invest a couple more days at Table of

Hope. This duty assignment had morphed into a service mission. Oddly, that didn't bother him too much. Observing people helping one another was interesting. This whole charity thing was a different way of looking at behavior, something that had never been of the slightest interest to Heath. He'd find a way to recycle the experience, make something useful out of it.

"Yeah, right," he huffed aloud. "Doing community service in a homeless shelter will contribute so much to my résumé when I'm job hunting on the West Coast."

"Stone, is that you?" Amos's voice sounded stronger.

Heath rounded the corner to find the old man propped up against the cushions of the sofa bed. His face was scruffy with several days of growth and his cheeks were hollow from losing a few pounds the hard way. But Amos's eyes were clear, a good sign that the fever was gone. Maybe he was past being contagious.

"Hey, man. You're lookin' better." Heath kept his voice low so they wouldn't wake Bruce and Nick.

"Any view of me besides curled up on the bathroom floor is bound to be an improvement." Amos chuckled, which set off a fit of coughing.

Heath grabbed a king-size bottle of cough

suppressant, filled a plastic spoon and passed it to Amos. Seconds later, with the bout under control, he took a sip of water from the cup Heath offered. A big sigh escaped as Amos dragged a damp cloth over his face, then looked up to where Heath stood nearby.

"I owe you an apology, Stone."

"For what?"

"For being hateful and judgmental when you first got here."

"I didn't even notice."

"That's because we're cut from the same cloth. We're self-centered, don't care much about other people's feelings."

Heath kept his face passive, not wanting the other man to see that his insult had hit the mark.

"I don't know how you can say that about yourself, Amos. You spend your days helping Olivia run this place."

"I'm not helping Miss Livvy—she's helping me. She put a roof over my head and gave me a chance to get on my feet. All she asked in return is that I come to Bible study and stay away from the booze."

"You're an alcoholic?" Heath settled into a chair beside the sofa.

"I was headed straight for it and didn't have any reason to do otherwise. But now that I'm sober my daughter wants me to come live with her in Houston."

"Does Olivia know?"

"Not yet. I didn't get a chance to tell her before this creepin' crud hit me. Now I think I'll save it for a Thanksgiving surprise."

"Unless things are a hundred percent better by then, I don't think the lady can take any more surprises."

Amos nodded slowly, as if movement would jump-start the coughing again.

"Can you make it down the steps? I thought you might like to take a shower and get back to your own bed."

"We're not worried about exposing our clients anymore?"

"The fifth person came down with it in the past hour so Olivia's closed the doors and worked out a deal with another shelter to help out for a few days."

Amos shut his eyes, pushed forward and then slumped back again. "I want to get up and help Miss Livvy but my body's dead weight."

"I don't doubt it," Heath sympathized. "You're wrung out from fever and stomach flu. The only way you can help Olivia is by taking it easy so you don't relapse. That's the last thing she needs."

Amos's lips gathered tight like the closing of a

drawstring bag. He looked hard at Heath. "You're sweet on her, aren't you?"

Did it show? How could that be? Heath hardly even knew what being *sweet on* somebody meant, let alone being sure that's how he felt.

"Olivia's a nice lady."

"She's just a girl, up to her eyeballs in work. She doesn't need the distraction of another heartache," Amos said archly.

"We are in complete agreement, *sir.*" Heath felt like he was being dressed down by somebody's daddy.

Commendable. But annoying. And unnecessary!

"Glad to hear it, *son,*" Amos said, tossing the insult back. "She talks a good game, and she even believes it. But you could drive a Mack truck through that hole in her spirit."

"You mind telling me what that means?"

Amos looked around as if they were in a crowded room where the pictures had ears. In a way that was true. Bruce and Nick hadn't flinched a muscle, but that didn't mean they weren't awake and listening.

"I don't suppose it'd be breakin' a confidence to mention her big shot daddy. When Dalton Wyatt ran off, it was all over the news in this neck of the woods. The Feds were worried about recovering money and locking Wyatt up. Nobody much cared that he'd abandoned a teenage daughter, left her to manage on her own."

"Didn't she have any family to take her in?"

"If she did, they were afraid of guilt by association and steered clear. Nope, she's self-made the hard way."

"She seems accomplished and sure of herself."

"Don't let that pretty exterior fool you. If it wasn't for having her nose in a Bible at night, she might not make it through each day. She's tough on the outside but her heart is tender. The residents are her strays. Miss Livvy takes us in and loves us, gives us a chance life says we don't deserve. I'm certain her intentions are in the right place, but I think we're just a substitute for a man in her life she can trust completely. A man worthy of her faith."

Nick began to stir, needed help getting to the bathroom. The conversation was over, but only for the moment. Heath needed to know more about Amos's insight.

So he could know more about Olivia's motivation.

Chapter Twelve

"I'm conflicted," Olivia announced to Heath that night when they finally took a break and settled in the big room, just the two of them.

"How's that?"

"I'm torn between groaning and yawning and too tired to do either one." She leaned her head back against the old tweed sofa and plopped her stocking feet on the scarred coffee table. "Serving dinner to a room full of hungry folks is definitely less stressful than caring for a handful of sick people."

"It's a good thing you went into social work and not health care."

"Ain't that the truth," she agreed.

"Why don't you turn in for the night?" Heath encouraged. "Your place has been aired out, wiped down and mopped up. It's ready when you are."

She rolled her head against the soft cushion to take in the amazingly kind man sitting to her left. He'd put in a grueling day and never uttered the words of complaint that had crossed her own lips a time or two. Their hours together had been a jigsaw puzzle experience. The more she knew about him, the more the pieces snapped into place. Heath Stone was a mystery wrapped around a contradiction, but his motives were sincere.

A woman could love a man like that. More importantly, she could trust and respect him.

"You've definitely repaid your debt to society and then some. How can I show my gratitude for your kindness, Heath?"

"You can tell me something about your residents."

Olivia felt her heavy eyelids open wide. Why in the world... "Most guys would take a very different approach to a woman offering to show her appreciation."

"You really want me to act like most guys?"

"Not at all." She shook her head, sorry she'd voiced the thought. "I just figured you'd want me to call Detective Biddle and tell him you've been working around the clock and deserve to be out of here and home before Thanksgiving."

He squinted, his eyes the color of wet driftwood. "Why do you continue to think I'm in a hurry to get away from here?"

"Oh, because a hundred miles up the road you have a life and a job and a home of your own. Anyone would be anxious to have community service over and done with so they could get back to normal."

"Well, that's where your theory breaks down. I don't know that I've ever had anything *normal* or even close enough to normal that I'm anxious to get back to it."

Since their first night he'd revealed bits and pieces about his past. He seemed to be inviting her to bring it up again.

"From what you've mentioned about your adoptive parents, it seems like life with them was an average American experience, no?"

He drew both shoulders to his ears and scrunched up his face.

She couldn't help snickering over the comic picture he made. His eyes were so expressive, communicating with glances what he couldn't or wouldn't say with words. "So, what does *that* mean?" She mirrored his silly posture.

"It means that whether or not my experience was average depends on your point of reference. My friends hung out at our house all the time so they must have felt welcome—by my mom anyway."

"Sounds like normal guy stuff."

"Yeah, but I would see my dad off to the side with his arms folded, constantly sizing everybody up as if he didn't approve. It was like he was always on the watch for somebody who would bring out the worst in me."

"Or maybe he just wanted you to have positive influences, Heath." How different her life might have been if her own father had been paying that kind of attention. Instead, he was busy cooking up a second set of books to keep the IRS off his trail. Obviously, he hadn't done a very good job of that, either. "Your dad was more engaged than most men are these days, and that certainly deserves appreciation."

"Speaking of appreciation, let's get back to our original discussion." Heath pushed off the sofa and moved toward the coffee station where he filled two cups with hot water and dunked a tea bag into each one. "You wanted to show yours, so I asked you to tell me about the residents. How about starting with Amos? He's an interesting character."

Heath returned to the sofa and handed her a warm mug fragrant with the aroma of Earl Grey.

"I thought you didn't care for Amos."

"He didn't care for me," Heath corrected as he fiddled with the string dangling from the mug.

"But he apologized earlier when I was helping him move back downstairs, so I'm interested in knowing more about Oscar the Grouch."

Olivia smiled at the apt description of the man she'd quickly grown to love. "Amos was the first resident I accepted into the program. He used to be a Houston cop."

Heath's chin snapped up. *"Really?"* The color of his eyes intensified at the revelation. "How long ago?" he asked.

"I think it's been fifteen years or more. He left voluntarily right after his marriage broke up. The application indicated he'd tried his hand at several trades but never found anything else that suited him."

"Why'd he leave the force?"

"You'll have to ask Amos. I ran a background check to verify his information. It was all straightforward and the interview went well so I accepted him for an indefinite period. He's been a huge help to me, though I have to admit he's probably run off a volunteer or two with his grumpy nature."

"How dare you talk about my new buddy that way," Heath said with a wry laugh.

She joined in the chuckle, knowing her suspicion about Amos was likely the truth. But losing the odd volunteer now and again was a fair trade for a grandfather figure who was so protective of her and Table of Hope.

"He looks out for me the same way he would his own kin if they'd have anything to do with him. As far as I'm concerned, this is Amos's home now, and for as long as he can stand to live out of a three-drawer chest beside his bunk."

Olivia's gaze locked with Heath's. "I'm glad to hear Amos apologized to you. He has a good heart, but he's socially awkward and judges too quickly. Maybe that's why he was unsuccessful as a cop."

Heath frowned and squirmed in his chair. He shifted his attention to his cup of tea and kept his eyes downcast, as if he'd taken her comment about Amos personally.

"What about the others?" He changed the subject.

Olivia spent the next hour sharing the lowdown on her small group of residents, but holding back anything she felt was confidential. Each person had a part-time job, paid a few dollars a day to live at Table of Hope and helped out with anything she needed when they were under her roof. Heath's interest in her friends had a warming effect on Olivia's spirit, as if the dancing flames in the room's painted-on fireplace had sprung to life.

He asked thoughtful questions, encouraged her

to share stories. His self-absorption was wearing away. Heath had a caring spirit, no matter how many strings of barbed wire he'd wrapped around his life to block out the world's touch. She knew firsthand about keeping her guard up. Some days it had been necessary to her very survival. But any form of armor eventually became inadequate once the heart was involved. She'd realized as he'd driven away in the old Chevy truck today that her heart was definitely and hopelessly involved.

Heath watched emotions cross Olivia's face as she spoke of the residents, people who were like family to her. She seemed clueless that somebody was passing drugs through her operation. How could she be blind to this after all she'd been through or naive in spite of what she'd accomplished?

His cop's voice of reason struggled for power. *Maybe her innocence is by design, you lovesick idiot. Women have been deceiving men since the Garden of Eden, right?*

Olivia smiled as she spoke, her dark eyes flashing when she shared some anecdote he couldn't hear for the thoughts churning in his head. Heath was convinced of what he'd said to Biddle. The lady was straight up, completely devoted to God and meeting the needs of others. No way would she knowingly give shelter to anyone living contrary to her mission.

In fact, Heath was pretty sure that if she realized he'd been lying from the get-go, she'd show him the toe of her boot right now. He doubted she'd even give him the chance to admit that his motives had shifted after the first twenty-four hours. His mission was no longer focused on indicting a stranger—it was about clearing the name of the woman he'd come to care for deeply.

"This timing couldn't be worse," Olivia was saying. "One more day of rounding up donations and some food club shopping would have covered us through the end of the month. With more freezing weather on the way, getting through the holiday is going to be dicey."

"Where, specifically, do you need to go?" Maybe she'd repeat the important parts he'd tuned out. "Can you cover everything in one day if you have my help?"

She heaved a sigh in response. "I'm not comfortable leaving my guys by themselves when they're still pretty weak."

"What about finding some more volunteers?"

"Between getting My Brother's Keeper to take all our clients, asking Grace Chapel to look after Velma and Erica, folks all over town hunkering down for bad weather and with the holidays coming, we've tapped out our emergency resources."

"Leave that to me."

"Who do you know in this town who's willing to give us a day of their time with no notice to care for people with the flu?"

"How about the man who convinced you to let me work off my community service?"

"Detective Biddle?" She smiled, warming to the idea. "Now that you mention it, he did say if I needed anything to holler."

"Maybe he'll send over that traffic cop who was eyeing you like a buzzard looks at a baby bunny."

"Oh, please." She lowered her face but couldn't hide the flush that kissed her collarbone and crept upward.

"You can deny it till the cows come home, but a man knows how to spot these things," he insisted.

"You're making too much out of an old friend's kindness."

Heath huffed at the insistence. "Let me put it this way—if I'd been Officer Weatherford, I'd have exchanged that *kindness* for your phone number."

She glanced up, her eyes round and surprised,

her lips pressed together with uncertainty. "Are you serious?"

"Serious as global warming. I knew what he was up to so I gave him the stink eye and scared him off. You can thank me for it later."

"I'll add that to the long list of things I have to repay you for some day."

"You don't have to repay me for anything. But you do have to get upstairs and get some rest. Let me take care of this place tonight, okay?"

She leaned forward on the sofa and reached for the worst excuse for boots Heath had ever seen. Nothing more than thick socks sewn over hunks of tire tread.

"I can't believe you paid good money for those." He motioned toward her feet where she was pulling the black-and-white-striped things almost to her knees.

"They were donated and it was my good fortune to have the only size 10 tug boats big enough to fill them." She pointed a toe and admired her foot. "Much warmer and more practical than stilettos. They're called UGGs."

"Well, I'd call 'em *ug-ly,* like that cap you wore yesterday. Those things remind me of—"

"Let me guess," she interrupted. "Something your mama used to wear."

"When she walked the dog in the rain."

"Then she must have been a very fashion-conscious woman."

"Just like you," he teased, knowing better. Olivia's casual style was appealing, not at all fussy. It was one more on the growing list of things that made her so attractive, that made it harder to keep reminding himself why he was here.

"Yeah, right." She slanted a skeptical glance his way and then exaggerated a supermodel strut toward the door. Turning in a circle she gave him a good look at her red thermal shirt and patched jeans and then she marched close enough to make him edge backward.

"Don't be doin' that for Officer Weatherford, okay?"

She stopped a couple feet in front of Heath, raised her arms slowly with hands clasped and stretched toward the ceiling. A small groan escaped as she enjoyed the motion of pulling the tension out of her muscles.

He placed fingertips on either side of her waist, turned her around and gave her a slight push away toward the exit.

Her fisted hands flew to her sides as she spun to face him. Her brows arched like punctuation over the confusion on her face. "Why'd you do that?"

Was there any chance she didn't know how she was affecting him?

"Because if you keep prancing around in front of me, I might behave like most guys after all."

A sly smile slid across her lips. She took a step closer. "I don't think so."

He took a step back. The heel of his shoe brushed the wall. He was as good as pinned. "Well, think again."

Sleek dark hair in need of a trim whisked across her eyelashes as she shook her head. "Your mama and daddy raised a gentleman, albeit a cantankerous one."

"And the more cantankerous I get, the more I need to have things my way."

"Okay, you get your way," she huffed, giving up the playful advance. "I don't want to end the day aggravating my favorite caregiver after all you've done, especially when there's more to do tomorrow."

She inched away. *Don't let her go,* his soul cried out. Heath covered the few feet between them, moved close enough to feel Olivia's breathing. He slid his hands around her waist and pulled her body near, relished her warmth.

Her eyes were wide, like shiny black jewels in a porcelain doll's face. She settled her palms against his chest. He held his breath, afraid she'd push away. Her lips curved into a smile that touched his heart. Her fingers slid around his neck, laced behind his head and without hesitation she pulled his mouth down to accept the sweet kiss she offered.

Chapter Thirteen

Olivia couldn't believe her boldness. It had to be the sheer fatigue taking over. If not for the feel of Heath's lips on hers, she'd suspect it was all a dream. A man hadn't kissed her since… Well, since longer than she wanted to remember. And *never* like this.

His body was warm and strong but undemanding. She'd initiated the dance and he was letting her lead. She pressed close, he pulled her tighter. She ran her fingers over his short crop of hair, he spread his palms against her waist.

He tasted like Earl Grey, smelled of Lysol.

He was wonderful.

And then as unexpectedly as it began, the kiss was over.

Heath dropped his hands to his sides and cleared his throat. She took it as an indication that he was uncomfortable and a sure sign they should call it a night.

The awkward moment was her fault. She had to smooth it over. Olivia gave in to the nervous fit of giggles that threatened to escape. The sound bubbled past her lips.

"Something funny?" He narrowed his eyes at her laughter.

"I don't know what's come over me," she snorted.

His eyes widened. "It's called delirium."

Heath clasped her hand in his, led her out of the big room, around the corner and through her colorful hallways. While she continued to snicker uncontrollably, he fished her door keys out of his pants pocket and unlocked her private stairwell.

"Here." He placed the keys in her palm. "When I finally settle down for the night it'll be right next to this door."

"No." She shook her head. "Please don't spend another night uncomfortable on my account. I only keep a watch posted at this door in case somebody needs to get inside after we're locked up. I don't have any security fears."

Not with you close by.

Olivia checked herself before the thought turned to words. She'd been crazy to initiate that kiss, and Heath had mercifully let her off the hook without embarrassment. The last thing she needed to do was voice a comment that made her sound needy. Or worse, assuming.

"Olivia, listen to me. You give the folks who stay under your roof far too much credit. When people are desperate, they will do desperate things."

"I appreciate the reminder, Heath. But I'm aware of the hazards of running a shelter. I try to use good judgment and take precautions, but I've learned to leave what's beyond my ability to God. He's my shield and my comfort. I trust Him completely."

She expected Heath to turn away, dismiss her statement. Instead, he seemed to be listening more closely, staring more intensely, as if her words were soaking in.

"I'm not sure it's wise to ever trust anyone completely."

She had to smile. "God's not *anyone,* Heath. He's the Creator of all things, the Alpha and the Omega. His Word endures forever."

"Okay." Heath dragged out the word. Maybe she'd lost him.

She pulled the door wide and stepped inside the lighted stairwell. She took two steps upward, hesitated and then glanced back. "Heath, something about leaving you down here by yourself just doesn't feel right."

"That's fatigue talking," he reassured her.

"You'll let me know if you need anything, right?"

"You can count on it."

Heath waited till he heard Olivia turn the dead bolt. He shut the security door and went to work, anxious to search the main level without interruption.

All was quiet in the men's dorm with Amos, Bruce and Nick in their bunks. Since Mary Sue had bid goodnight and locked the door to the women's quarters well over an hour ago, Heath presumed she was down for the count, as well.

He crept from room to room, closet to closet, using Olivia's spare set of keys to explore. He found two more vacuum-sealed bags brimming with green pills—one among the laundry supplies and the other in the far corner of a staples pantry.

At half-past midnight, Heath sat alone in the dining room, making notes of what he knew to be facts, looking for the common denominator. *Olivia.* She was the only one who totally made sense and his heart was heavy at the thought. If the DEA had searched Table of Hope tonight, she could be on her way to jail. Charges might not stick, but the damage would be done.

Heath lowered his face, pressed his forehead against his palms.

"Lord, I've got to find a way to protect her from this mess. Please give me some help here."

"I doubt I'm your first choice, but I can listen to whatever's eatin' on you." A gravelly male voice ended Heath's brief plea.

Amos settled into the folding chair across the table. He swirled a spoon in a mug. Crackers were stacked on the edge of the saucer. "Broth," he explained. "I gotta get somethin' to stay inside my old body before I dry up and blow away."

"It's good to see you moving under your own steam." Heath was annoyed by the intrusion, but relieved to see Amos up and about.

"So, tell me what's got a heathen like you asking God for help?"

"I wouldn't exactly call myself a heathen." Heath took umbrage at the description his dad had used a time or two.

"Well, you won't pass for a choir boy, either, so we'll accept that you're somewhere in the middle."

"Thanks." That didn't feel any better. "Olivia tells me you used to be a cop."

Amos nodded, fixed Heath with a hard stare. "You in some kinda trouble?"

"No, but Olivia could be and I need another

person who cares for her as much as I do to help me out."

"Name it. I love that girl." Amos's voice was quiet, like he was worried he'd jinx himself if he admitted his protective feelings for Olivia too loudly.

Heath understood. He took a leap of faith.

"Amos, I'm going against conventional wisdom to trust you with something that could get us both shot. But being an ex-cop, I think you'll want to help out."

A smile deepened the crags of the old man's face. He grunted, crumbled a cracker into his cup, picked up his spoon and motioned for Heath to get on with the story.

The little hand on the kitchen clock was just past six when Heath glanced up to find Olivia in the doorway. The look of wonder on her face made him send up a silent prayer of thanks. He couldn't recall even a Christmas morning that had been any more fun.

"What is going on in here?" Her gaze roamed the room, taking in the newcomers who were preparing a hot but bland breakfast for their pitiful band of patients.

"Olivia, this is my bride of thirty-four years, Peggy." Biddle introduced his wife. "We're here for today and tomorrow and the next day if you need us."

"My Bill won't shy away from a job as long as somebody gives him direct orders. That's why I'm here," Peggy joked, sending a look of unbridled love toward her husband.

"I can't believe you're willing to come in contact with flu to help us out."

Peggy waved away Olivia's concern. "We take the shots every year and go about our business praying for the best. If the crud's gonna get you, the crud's gonna get you. And Bill never uses all his vacation days so this is a good excuse for us to spend some time together."

"Still…" Olivia seemed lost for words, more grateful even than Heath expected. "I don't know how to thank you for your kindness."

His heart thudded as a deep color rose in her face, emotional thoughts sparkled in her eyes. If he didn't get Olivia out of here, somebody was going to burst into tears, and that *somebody* was anybody's guess. He slapped his palms together, diverting attention from the red splotches on her cheeks.

"Everything's covered here. Let's go take care of the rest of your errands so we'll be ready for Thanksgiving."

"Hey, Stone," Biddle called and then tossed a set of keys. "Take our SUV. You'll be less likely to have a flat or need a push, and the backseat is down and ready for cargo."

Heath raised the keys in a salute, gave Olivia a gentle push out the kitchen door and grabbed his old quilted jacket off the coat hook.

Olivia felt like she was being courted. She sat in the window banquette of the sidewalk café several hours later while Heath fetched their cups of espresso and decadent orders of tiramisu. It was the closest thing to a date that she'd had since college. And even then it had been a Dutch treat with some guy from grad school who couldn't afford to pay attention, much less supersize her value meal.

Heath amazed her at every turn; insisting on opening doors, expertly handling the borrowed SUV, following her directions without question, doing all the manual work and then insisting on taking her out to lunch.

She watched him across the way, his expression impassive, just as it had been the first time they'd met. He was masterful at maintaining a poker face, holding any positive thoughts captive. He gave a curt nod to the cashier as she handed over his change. While he waited for the order to be prepared, he turned toward their table.

Their eyes locked, she smiled and his face transformed, like a dark mask had fallen away.

His shoulders relaxed as if he allowed himself to exhale for the first time that day. The tenseness in Heath's jaw eased and the tightness in his lips faded. A boyish grin appeared where the flat line of his lips had been. Lips that had touched her own. Lips she could kiss forever.

I care deeply for Heath. Her heart rattled hard, painful as she turned the thought over in her mind. But it was more and she knew it.

Lord help me, but I love him!

Olivia sucked in a breath and held it, afraid the admission would escape into the atmosphere along with the whoosh of air. For the first time in her adult life, she looked at a man through the eyes of love. Panic began to rise up from her core.

Her spirit cried out, *Father, do I dare hope for this relationship to have a future? Heath and I have both overcome great loss, so we're not so different. But the way we've chosen to respond has our lives on rails headed in opposite directions. I don't believe You would bring him into my life just to teach me one more lesson about letting go. Please, Lord, let my witness show Heath the joy of holding tight to You.*

As Olivia's desperate plea ended, Heath crossed toward her, set the tray on the table and folded his long, lean body into the low chair. He served her first and then himself.

"How about telling me what you were thinking just now?" He tore open two sugar packets at the same time and upended them into his demitasse.

"Why do you ask?" She scooped the dollop of whipped cream off her dessert and floated it atop her espresso.

"Because ten seconds ago there was a pretty smile on your face and now you look like your picnic is about to be rained out."

She was tempted to give him a truthful response, to share her overwhelming sense of both love and fear. But she needed time to analyze the unfamiliar feelings. Tomorrow would be soon enough to share her heart, and if tomorrow never came then she'd trust God to work it all out for His glory.

"I was just thinking about how similar we are." She hated only telling part of the truth.

"And that was so sad it made your face cave in?" As he cocked his head to one side and slanted an expectant look her way, he savored a spoonful of tiramisu.

She followed his lead and dug into her dessert. "Umm," she moaned, her eyes closed as she delighted in the rich flavors.

"Come on, answer the question," he insisted. "Am I so awful that it bothers you to have something in common with me?"

"Oh, of course not, Heath."

She rested her spoon on the plate and then wrapped her fingers around his wrist. The skin was warm where her cool fingertips met his flesh. He cupped his other hand over hers, the heat from his gentle touch settling like a treasured quilt over her soul.

"Then please explain."

"In our own way we're each orphans."

"Huh." He huffed the one-syllable response. "Hadn't thought about it that way, but I guess you're right."

"And I was wondering why God let both of us experience tragedy so early in life."

He gave her hand a squeeze. "You don't need to feel sorry for me. I wouldn't call my circumstances *tragic*. Yeah, it's awful that I was separated from my birth family, but that hardly compares to your situation. Losing your mom and then your dad running off. That's just wrong. A man's supposed to take care of his family, you know?" Heath bobbed his head. A look of disgust knitted his brows together. "But see how far we've both come?" he reminded her as he shook off the moment of melancholy by pulling his hand away and turning his attention back to their dessert. "We finished college and got stable jobs, not bad in this economy."

"But you said my potential is limited." She cared what he thought.

"Like a lot of my comments, that one came out all wrong. I meant your *earning* potential, but I have an idea for how you can have your tiramisu and eat it, too. And all to benefit the people you support at Table of Hope." He smiled, clinked his small cup to hers and raised it to his lips with a wink of a dark brown eye. The man was being downright playful.

"Oh, really?" What harm was there in going along with him? "Tell me more, please."

"I can do better than that. Drink up and I'll show you."

Chapter Fourteen

"The warehouse club is that way." Olivia pointed east.

Heath continued on his westward journey, excitement building over the brainstorm that he hoped Olivia would call a *God thing*. If Heath was right, this could open doors to her amazing talent and create a nice revenue stream for the shelter as a byproduct. "Did I say we were headed directly to the warehouse club?"

"No, but that's where we need to be going, and soon." She tapped on the SUV's dashboard clock. "It's getting late and we have groceries to buy."

"I promise we'll finish all your errands so just sit back and enjoy the detour. It's only about fifteen minutes out of the way and it'll be time well spent."

"It's bad enough that we took an hour for

lunch, Heath. We really need to get back to the shelter to relieve the Biddles. What if they need something?"

Heath reached into the center console and produced a black leather case containing a cell phone. "Detective Biddle told me he left this in the car on purpose. He can reach us if anybody has a problem."

"I just don't know about this. I'm not comfortable wasting time while others take care of my business."

"Then let's not waste the time. We skipped Bible study last night so why don't you give me a dose right now?"

Olivia whipped her head to the left. Her indigo eyes were wide, assessing. "Are you making fun of me?"

"I never get the benefit of the doubt with you, do I?" He shot an exaggerated look of exasperation in her direction. "Is it any wonder my glass is half-empty?"

Olivia turned her face left and right, taking in the surroundings. "I haven't figured out where we're headed yet and I grew up in this town. Shouldn't we be using that thing?" She pointed to the fancy built-in GPS.

He tapped his index finger against his temple. "I have an uncanny sense of direction. Trust me, boss lady. We're not a couple of lost sheep."

"What a perfect setup." She straightened in the seat, a gleam in her eyes as if a brilliant idea had struck. "I have a favorite story from the Gospel of John if you seriously want to hear it."

"The floorboard's all yours." He swept his palm, a sign to take it away.

Olivia shared the story of Jesus being the good shepherd, the one way to the Father.

"Isn't that *one-way* business the reason people criticize Christians for being narrow-minded?"

"Narrow thinking is not the same as the way to the Father being narrow. Every religion has a pathway that claims to lead to righteousness, but it's always paved with works and efforts to earn favor."

"But my mom always told me faith without works is dead."

"That's because what we do for others is our response to mercy. We serve out of gratitude, not fear or some effort to win eternal brownie points."

Heath turned his head as if looking for an upcoming street sign. In truth he was taking a moment to let Olivia's explanation take root.

"Olivia, do you think we only get one chance to take God up on that grace offer?"

He felt the pressure of her hand on his arm. Warmth seeped through his jacket and into his skin where she squeezed tightly.

"Heath, He never gives up on us. Christ wants to save every last one of His lost sheep. And that's exactly why I love the story of the Good Shepherd."

A knot of anxiety thickened Heath's throat. He'd been lost all his life, in so many ways. He exhaled loudly trying to free the stress along with the breath from his lungs. How incredible to have new mercy each day no matter how little he deserved it.

"Did I say too much?" There was worry in her voice.

He flipped on his right blinker and pulled to the side of the road, coming to a stop against the curb. His heart told him this moment was important, deserved eye-to-eye conversation.

"Everything you've said from the time we met until just now has been what I needed to hear. I've always understood with my head, and we know that's a skeptical place. I never let it sink down into my heart, until just now."

She rested a gloved hand along his jaw, her eyes glittering as brightly as her smile.

"If this is what your mission is all about, then I believe your potential is unlimited."

"Thank you for saying that, Heath," Olivia whispered.

Thank You for opening my eyes, Lord, Heath prayed.

Rising from his core was a desperate need to pull her into his arms, bury his face against her gosh-ugly stocking cap and kiss the crown of her head. But this intimate time was not about intimacy. He wanted Olivia to be certain that he knew the difference.

"Now, back to our road trip, Miss Livvy."

A small frown puckered her brow. "You're the only person who calls me by my full name these days, and I like hearing it. Would you mind?"

"Not at all, *Olivia.*" He angled his head in salute. He loved her name, and everything about her.

Far too much.

Heath checked the side mirror and blended the SUV into traffic. Best to put the hands that itched to hold her on the steering wheel and keep the thoughts that wanted to run wild under control.

"How about finding us some tunes?" he asked.

While she fiddled with the radio dial, it gave him a moment to think, to calm the thumping in his chest. This assignment needed to be wrapped up, quickly. If the plan he and Biddle initiated today panned out, things would be kicking into high gear very soon. Then he'd be free to get on with a new life.

Once the weight of undercover worry was off his mind, he could reach out to his oldest sister and tell her why he'd ignored her letters. In his backpack was another envelope from San Angelo with a fresh postmark, still unopened. She was unusually persistent.

Like Olivia.

Heath watched a smile touch her eyes as she found a station that pleased her. He'd give just about anything to please her for a lifetime.

What if I tell her the truth? The thought was appealing.

And which truth would that be, you big liar? He scolded himself. The whole time she'd been sharing her heart with him he'd been making up one story after another, saying anything to get the job done. The only time he'd been completely honest was a few minutes ago.

No, it was out of the question. He wouldn't sacrifice the trust she'd learned to give others so he'd benefit. Especially when there was a stronger-than-average chance she couldn't forgive his deceptions.

Better to stick with the plan than launch into the unknown with no strategy at all.

"Hey, I recognize where we are, now. That Jack and Jill's bakery makes the best doughnuts in Waco. And over there is an art gallery that I visited a few times when I was a kid." Olivia mentioned it moments before Heath pulled into a fifty-yard-line spot near the front entry. "I haven't been here since before my mother died."

"You know this place, huh?"

"It's one of the nicest in this part of the state." She sounded impressed. "They have a reputation as a launchpad for local artists."

"That's a good enough recommendation for me. Let's take a look inside."

Heath climbed out of the SUV and rounded the front bumper to get Olivia's door. He grasped her hand to help her to the ground, letting go reluctantly. He allowed himself to sweep an arm behind her protectively, blocking the cold wind as they crossed the few feet to the entrance.

The bell above the door jingled when they rushed inside, stamping their feet against the freezing temperature.

"Come on in here where it's warm!" A forty-ish man with a goatee stepped from behind a counter in the back of the store and approached with a smile. "My name's Lance. What can I do for you folks today?"

"We needed a break from cabin fever." Heath stepped up to offer his hand. "I'm Heath and this is my friend, Olivia. Mind if we take a look around?"

"I'll be offended if you don't. Just give a yell if you have questions."

Olivia left Heath's side, eager to explore. She

wandered among the paintings, admiring the work of artists talented enough to be displayed in a professional gallery. She'd never even have the boldness to show at the community art festival, much less a place like this.

She slowed before a wall of figurative paintings, the humanlike images blurred and blended into their activities; a dancer became one with the mirror, a cellist's bow ended where the musician's arm began. Olivia turned slowly, encircled by the light, color, texture and perspective.

"I so admire the hard work it takes to hone talent like this. Someday I hope to paint at this level."

His palm pressed against her shoulder to get her attention. His touch ignited a spark that chased away the chill in her core. She angled her face upward so their eyes met.

"Sweet lady, you're not only certifiably crazy, you're blind as a newborn jackrabbit. How can you see the potential in other people and miss it in yourself?"

She ducked her chin, fiddled with the zipper pull on her heavy jacket. His knuckle brushed the underside of her jaw, tipped her head back.

"Olivia, folks aren't just being nice when they make a fuss over your murals at Table of Hope. When I first saw them, I was sure some professionals had agreed to donate their work just so they could use it as a write-off."

"There you go, thinking the worst."

"Exactly!" He threw up both hands. "Your painting is so amazing that I never thought for a minute to give credit to an amateur."

"So, we agree. I'm an amateur. What's your point here?"

He took her by the hand and tugged her across the hall to an empty display space marked with a RESERVED placard. The walls were bare and waiting to be hung with vivid canvases that would fetch good prices from collectors and decorators.

"My point is that you have an income source that needs to be tapped. Imagine what could be accomplished at Table of Hope if you boost your budget by selling your paintings."

She stiffened, began to back up from the very idea. But Heath squeezed the hand he still held, refused to let her pull away.

"You can't tell me you've never thought about this," he insisted. "Anybody with an artistic bent dreams about being successful at one time or another."

She wanted to stamp her boot, deny that his words were true. But she'd glanced at the canvases on her walls upstairs more than once and imagined the day they would hang in a gallery.

The foolish thought must have shown on her face. He pulled her closer, tucked her beneath his chin, and held her in the crook of his strong arm.

"It's nothing to be ashamed of, Olivia. Needing to be validated is human, and you keep telling me how much you've studied human nature so you already know what I'm trying to say. If your gift can help earn the money that lets you support the mission, how will it be a bad thing?"

He stepped in front of her, placed his palms on either side of her face, cupping her head gently. "You know that Bible verse about not hiding your light under a bushel basket?"

She nodded, her throat too clogged with emotion to speak.

"Well, there you go. Even God is on board with the plan."

"There's a plan?" she asked, closer each moment to losing her composure.

Heath nodded. "I hope you won't be angry with me for poking my big nose into your business." He led her to a nearby bench where they sank down together, shoulders touching companionably.

"When you loaned me your truck the other day I smuggled one of your paintings over here."

Olivia dropped her forehead into her hands, too embarrassed now for Heath to see her face.

"Which painting?" she mumbled through her fingers.

"The one with the sun setting over the suspension bridge. It looks so much like a sinking ball of fire you can almost hear the Brazos hissing. I brought it to Lance, the guy we saw up front. His folks own this place. He said that if the rest of your work is that good he'd like to have a private showing for you and the sooner the better. They'll invite designers who like to get in on the ground floor with new artists. Lance was pretty excited when we talked. He said collectors will be anxious to buy before Christmas."

"Heath, I don't know what to say. I need some time to digest this news."

"You don't have to say anything." He placed his hand on the small of her back, rubbed lightly in circles as one would with an anxious child. "You're not obligated to do anything. If this doesn't appeal to you, then chuck the whole idea. I just thought maybe you and that old Chevy of yours had something in common."

Heath leaned over and pushed his shoulder against hers. "You know what I mean? Needing a little nudge to get you movin' on your own," he teased.

She dropped her hands from her face, returned his goofy smile and leaned into the arm he held open in invitation.

"What do you say we go talk to Lance and invite him to drop by tomorrow?"

"Yeah, like he wants to visit the flu zoo."

"If it's necessary, Lance can come in the side door and climb straight upstairs. And if the others are better when we get back, he won't even need to do that. Besides, he ought to see your murals. I'm sure rich ladies would pay you big bucks to liven up their boring dining rooms with rain forests and waterfalls. Where did you learn to do that, anyway?"

"I'm self-taught. After my dad left, I painted the boring dining rooms of my rich neighbor ladies and they paid my utilities in exchange." She smiled at the memory of her early efforts.

"Then I'd say you already have a toehold in the Waco art scene. Now, how's that for positive thinkin'?"

Chapter Fifteen

On the trip back to the shelter, Heath was glad to be at the wheel of his big Jeep again. Biddle's idea to drive it over and "loan" it for the day had been a good one. The last thing Heath wanted was to spend hours climbing in and out of Olivia's freezing old truck. Even with the vintage heater cranked up high, you could still see your breath inside the cab.

In the passenger seat beside him, Olivia sneezed. It was a girly sound that turned his reserve to mush and set him to worrying. She'd managed to dodge the flu bullet and didn't need to be flirting with an earache or a head cold.

"God bless you." Heath meant it with all his heart.

She was snuggled deep into her coat with both arms folded close across her chest. She sneezed again. He pointed to the box of tissues he always kept in the console, a habit he'd picked up from his mom. He was giving her more credit every day for the good sense in his life.

"You warm enough? Don't sit in a heap over there shivering in silence."

"I'm not." Her body language shifted. She grabbed a tissue, dabbed at her nose and then relaxed her hands into her lap.

"I guess I was physically hugging the day to myself."

"In a good way?"

"In a very good way," she assured him.

"I'm glad you aren't mad at me about the gallery thing."

"How could I be mad? Heath, nobody's ever cared enough to go to bat for me as you just did. I mean, I had an advisor in college who helped me through all the red tape of applying for grants and loans because she knew I was on my own, but that was her job. You took it upon yourself to help me get this opportunity and now I'm even deeper in your debt."

He dismissed her gratitude with a shrug and then adjusted the thermostat.

"I'm just payin' it forward." Another half truth, a lie by any other name. Yes, he needed to start giving back the kindness he'd been shown, but mostly he wanted to make up for some of the lack in Olivia's life. Lack she didn't even recognize because her glass was always half-full.

She'd made the most of a terrible situation while he'd been complaining about the best adoptive parents a kid could hope for. What must his sisters have experienced going from one foster home to the next when he'd been with a family who wanted him? He'd been an ungrateful jerk and that's all there was to it. He had fences to mend, sins to repent for, bridges to build, and he was ready to get started.

"Being at your place with people who are in serious need has been an eye-opener," he confessed to Olivia. "For all my griping, I've had it pretty easy. If I have even one compassionate bone in my body I hope it's not so brittle that it can't be rehabilitated."

"Well, I'm grateful that God's not only let me witness your change of heart, He's put me on the receiving end of your payback efforts."

Heath held his palm outward, shielding himself from the praise. "Olivia, trust me when I tell you that I don't deserve your kind words. It was time for me to wake up and smell the coffee cake. This is a season for family and I need to make amends with my parents. I'm ashamed to admit that I don't even know what they have planned for Thanksgiving. I have to give them a call."

She nodded but didn't speak for a long while,

looking out the window at the passing cars. He saw her swipe the back of her hand at her face where something bothered her cheek. That *something* left a trail that gleamed when the sun glinted through the windshield.

Oh, man! I just had to go running off at the mouth about kinfolk when the people at Table of Hope are the only family Olivia's got and they're all sick. How am I going to fade out of the picture this time without looking back?

"Are you sure about this?"

Biddle nodded, agreeing that the plan they'd worked out while Heath was away would be the best way to go.

Heath looked from Biddle to Amos and back again. The three of them sat around a card table in the big room while Peggy was upstairs with Olivia giving a female opinion on her paintings.

"Amos is on board and I can't see dragging this out any longer." Biddle's mind seemed made up.

Heath looked to Amos for confirmation.

"I'll bet you're thinking I'm nothin' but a broken down old man. But I've had my proud moments. I'd like to believe I still have a few left in me."

"Amos, if you're thinking of sacrificing

yourself for Olivia, don't go there. I'll find a way
to protect her."

"You know there's nothin' I wouldn't do for
Miss Livvy, but this is bigger than her reputation
or even the good work that goes on here at Table
of Hope. I was a beat cop for over twenty years.
I left because I was sick of ringing doorbells at
night to notify mamas and daddies that their kids
were DOA at the hospital thanks to recreational
drugs. Some party, huh?"

Amos closed his eyes for a few long seconds,
like the memories were too harsh to face. Heath
considered how his law enforcement path compared to Amos's. Amos left because his heart
wouldn't harden, then never found another place
where he belonged. By contrast Heath's ticker
was so calloused over that he'd lost what little
empathy he might have had at one time. He just
didn't see any fulfillment in sticking with police
work. Worse still, he suspected he might eventually feel the same way sitting behind a desk in
Silicon Valley. Would it be different if he let God
direct his steps instead of leaning on his own
pitiful understanding?

"Heath." Biddle broke the silence. "If we get
the sick folks out of here pretty quick, the shelter can be back in business that much sooner.
The three of us working together can break this
case in the next seventy-two hours. With more

freezing weather on the way, our importers will be anxious to settle up and head for a warmer climate."

"But when word gets out that a WPD detective and his wife are volunteering here, that'll drive the action away." Heath challenged the logic.

"Exactly. Then we can finish this somewhere else and keep Table of Hope in the clear," Biddle explained.

"Makes sense," Heath agreed, then turned to Amos. "I'm glad you're on board with this. I thought about talking to you myself after Olivia told me you'd been a cop, but first I called Biddle in to check you out and make sure you weren't dirty. I hope you'll forgive me if that offends you."

Heath felt Biddle staring, knew the expression on his friend's face. It would be the same gaping look he'd given Heath the last time he'd said something remotely sensitive. That apology just now probably had Biddle's eyes bulging, but Heath wasn't gonna turn his head to find out.

Amos scratched at the stubble on his face. "No hard feelings. Any cop with good sense would do the same thing."

"You got any idea who our inside guy could be?" Heath changed the subject.

"Actually, I have suspicions about a lot of the

characters who come around here. But there is somebody in particular I keep my eye on."

Feminine chatter grew. The men exchanged glances and clammed up.

"In here, Miss Livvy," Amos called. His voice was stronger, and Heath noticed that the fits of coughing seemed less intense.

Olivia stepped through the doorway and her gaze locked briefly with Heath's. His insides shuddered. Even being apart for a short while made him anxious to see her.

Not worried anxious, hardly able to think anxious.

His mind ping-ponged on this new sensation, not at all convinced it was a good thing. Did matters of the heart pass as quickly as they struck? Or could this intensity possibly hang on, become constant?

Heath still remembered *the talk* during the summer he was fifteen. His dad confided that he fell in love with Heath's mama when they were in a college study group together. He claimed that after only a few weeks the longing in his heart was downright painful, made it impossible to function apart from her. He'd said, "That's how I knew she was the girl I'd waited for, the only one I'd ever want to share my life with." And today, even after thirty-seven years of marriage, Heath's parents couldn't bring themselves to spend a night apart.

He'd always thought their story was a bunch of baloney. But not anymore. Not since he'd experienced that same painful longing for himself.

I don't have any business being in love, Lord! Why me and why now?

Heath figured he'd find a nice woman one day, but never dreamed it would overpower him, and out of the blue like this. He wasn't ready. There had to be a way to distance himself from this feeling. It was too... Too everything!

Work was what he needed. He'd get his head back in the game and his heart would follow.

Wouldn't it?

"That's wonderful news!" Olivia shouted over Heath's thoughts. She was smiling, hugging the Biddles. They must have told her the only part of the plan that she could hear. In a couple more days they'd be able to reopen the shelter if all went well. She radiated with happiness. At the thought of serving others the woman was even more beautiful.

His heart was hosed.

"You do understand we have to relocate our sick folks till they're better."

"How is that going to happen?" Olivia asked Biddle.

Peggy answered for her husband. "When the

mayor heard how you were struggling to take care of a staff with flu and still keep homeless people out of this dangerous weather, he stepped in to get you some relief. Waco General is going to double up in private rooms until the epidemic is over. And the best part is they're going to start by taking in the cases you've been caring for so Table of Hope can get back to the business of being a shelter."

Olivia's mouth formed a silent and beautiful "O" as she stood with both hands clasped over her tender heart.

"Detective Biddle, are you the man I have to thank for carrying that message to City Hall?"

Biddle shrugged off the praise with a shake of his head. "I just mentioned it to the chief when I phoned to tell him I'd be taking a few days off to help out here. He took it from there."

Her eyes filled up and fat tears dribbled over Olivia's dark lashes. Heath glanced at Amos to the right and Biddle to the left. If he hadn't been trapped between the devil and the deep blue sea, Heath would wrap her in his arms and hold her heart next to his until the waterworks dried up.

Fortunately, Peggy stepped in. She flung a motherly arm around Olivia's waist and they leaned close.

"Let's get started, Miss Livvy." Amos, bless his heart, spoke up and broke the weepy spell.

"The bus will be here before we know it. I need to talk to Bruce and Nick about this and you have to get the ladies ready." He shuffled toward the hall.

"Are you going to the hospital with the others, Amos?" Worry resonated in Olivia's question.

"Not on your life. I'm sticking around here if you'll let me. I'm well enough to manage the laundry while we get the place cleaned up. Maybe Emeril over there can help out in the kitchen." Amos smirked and jerked his chin at Heath.

"Thanks for the nomination, but we all know I'm better with a plunger than a potato masher. Let's find another sucker for KP."

"If you need kitchen help, I'm the woman for the job." Peggy laughed as she volunteered.

"I look a little silly in pink rubber gloves, but my wife's taught me to do a fair job of scrubbing pots and pans." Biddle offered his services.

"You two don't mind staying on?" Olivia looked like the tears might flow again.

"Honey, it's no hardship for either of us." Peggy comforted Olivia with another hug. "We're blessed to be a blessing, so let us do what we can."

Heath stole a look at Biddle. The admiration in his eyes as he studied his wife was undeniable. Was it worth all the effort they gave to their marriage to have such a connection?

Was it truly worth risking everything to love like that?

Chapter Sixteen

For the first time in days, Olivia breathed a sigh of relief. Her friends would be in good hands at Waco General and she could start getting things at the shelter back to normal. She tucked sheets and smoothed blankets over the freshly sanitized beds in the women's dorm and pondered what *back to normal* meant now that a man had flipped her world on its ear.

How was it that her outlook could change so much in such a short time? She'd been content for years to take each day's trouble as it arrived, knowing there would always be plenty of problems. And now she was dreaming about possibilities for the future, definitely expecting good things to happen.

It was all because of Heath.

An uncomfortable thought struck, slowing Olivia's hands from their efforts. She'd been pointing out his negative way of thinking and all that time she hadn't really expected new blessings for herself! Oh, she had a positive attitude and perspective on life, but that was easy when you didn't set yourself up to be disappointed by people who had so little to give.

Heath had a rough way of looking at the world and maybe he was more right than she knew. But his toughness had turned out to be no deeper than his skin, and she loved that about him.

She loved everything about Heath Stone. But what was she supposed to do with that knowledge?

Pray!

Father, forgive me that I haven't been on my knees about this already. You alone have seen me through all the valleys in my life. How could I expect to be on a mountaintop and not share it with You? Thank You for bringing Heath into my comfortable little world to shake things up in a way I'd never have been brave enough to do on my own. Show me how to affect him in the same way, Lord. Give me the opportunity and the words to tell him how I feel in what little time we have left together.

"You seem to like him a lot. Does he know?"

Olivia's head snapped up, wondering if she'd uttered her silent prayer aloud.

"Excuse me?"

Peggy was on her knees, making up a nearby lower bunk. An indulgent smile made her face glow younger than her sixty-some-odd years. "I asked if you've told Heath how much you care about him."

Olivia ran her hand across the mattress, chasing wrinkles to buy time. She needed advice and with Velma gone there was no one to share girl talk. That was probably fortunate, since Peggy's guidance in the romance department would be more reliable than anything Velma might contribute on the subject.

"I understand if you don't want to answer my nosy question. It's none of my business anyway," Peggy apologized.

Olivia tucked one foot beneath her and dropped into a cross-legged position on a braided rug beside the bunk. She reached toward a basket of towels waiting to be folded.

"I don't mind your asking. In fact, I could use some guidance."

Peggy moved closer to help with the laundry. "So, you really are smitten with him, huh?"

Olivia nodded, still afraid to confess her heart out loud. "It's probably one-sided, but we did share a kiss the other night." It was too embarrassing to admit she'd initiated the intimacy. "Nothing's happened since."

"He seems like such a nice guy. Has he told you much about himself?" Peggy's soft voice was encouraging.

"Indirectly."

Peggy's brows tipped together and she cocked her head to one side. "How's that?"

"Heath's made some comments about being adopted as a small child but never really feeling connected to his parents. I think that's also the story of his religious experience."

"That he was adopted into it but never chose to be part of it?"

Olivia nodded. "Exactly. But in the past few days, I've seen him pick up the loose thread and start to weave God's presence into his thinking."

"I shouldn't be repeating what Bill's told me," she confided. "But my husband is a strong judge of character and he thinks Heath has more potential than what he's lived up to so far."

"Oh, you mean the Intranet prank that landed him here for community service." Olivia presumed. "He's so intense that I can't even imagine Heath wasting time doing something like that. It's out of character for the man I've gotten to know." She shrugged and reached for another towel. "But guys will do lots of stupid things on a dare."

"Tell me about it. In '79 Bill had to shave his head when the Cowboys lost the Super Bowl. I think my husband is the most handsome man on earth, but for those few weeks that he was bald I felt like I was married to a Conehead." Peggy laughed, a contagious sound that made Olivia join in until the fit of giggles ran its silly course.

"So, what are you going to do about Heath?" Peggy swiped at the tears of laughter that leaked down her face.

"That's where I need guidance. This place is my life." Olivia glanced around the women's quarters. "He has a home and a career in Austin. What's the point in telling him I care when he'll be gone the minute I sign his community service papers?"

"He doesn't live that far away."

"I'm not looking for a long-distance romance no matter what the mileage is, and I work 24/7 so my weekends aren't even available."

Peggy shrugged, both shoulders rising momentarily to meet her ears. "Given all that, I don't see where my advice would make a difference. Sounds like you've made up your mind already."

"Yeah." Olivia's agreement was like a weight on her chest. "I guess I have. And now with the possibility that I could show and sell some of my canvases, I really won't have two minutes to rub together."

"Then I'd say you should just take things as they come and trust God to work out His plans for both of you. Enjoy whatever time you have with Heath and if the moment seems right to share your heart, do it. No matter what the outcome is, don't be sorry for it."

Olivia nodded agreement. "Thank you, Peggy. I already have more 'what ifs' than the law allows. I don't need another one dragging me down."

"Woulda-shoulda-coulda's are dead weight, aren't they? I'll always regret that my daddy never said he loved our mother in front of us kids. We knew he did, of course, but he was from an era where real men didn't talk about emotional things. If I had it to do over, I'd press him to tell me how he felt about Mama so I'd have those words to treasure now that they're both gone."

Olivia understood only too well. There was precious little left of her past and she was busy with the present. All by herself. Thanks to Heath there was new promise for her future. If possibilities were all she had to remind her of Heath after he went home, then he'd given her a wonderful treasure indeed.

* * *

"Wanna take a ride, get some ice cream or a doughnut?" Heath waited nervously in the doorway to Olivia's office that night. He'd grabbed her heavy coat from the hall tree, and stood ready to help her into it. He had to be alone with her again. Had to have her undivided attention, at least for a while. His feelings were growing stronger by the minute and precious time was slipping away. A voice inside that he didn't recognize and couldn't explain was urging him on.

"You can't be serious." Olivia glanced up from the paperwork on her desk, then checked the time. "We just locked up for the night."

"So? That's the best part about running your own place. If you wanna take a break, there's nobody to stop you." He held up her coat in one hand, her scarf and familiar old cap in the other.

"What about Amos?"

"*What about him?* Do you honestly think he can't handle an empty building by himself for an hour?" Heath asked.

"Should we invite him to join us?" The tiniest grin twisted the corners of her mouth.

"Very funny." Heath dropped his arms by his sides, tipped his head to the left and bit back further comment while he waited for her to take him up on his offer. He wouldn't accept anything less than yes for an answer. "Look, let's go enjoy ourselves while we can. Tomorrow you'll be up before the chickens to get ready for a visit from the gallery guy and then you'll start cooking for Thanksgiving. I'll be busy from sunup to sundown on that to-do list of yours because I want to make as many of those repairs as I can before my time here runs out."

She stopped fiddling with the pencil in her right hand. Her lips pressed together, all sign of teasing gone. A crease settled between her dark brows as if a new worry wrinkle had moved into her brain.

"What is it, Olivia? Your whole face just went sad, like you got bad news."

"I realize there's something I need to take care of before it gets any later." She pushed up from her chair and reached toward Heath for her things. "I'll be ready to go as soon as I tell Amos we're leaving."

"He already knows, said have a nice time."

Heath watched her loop her knitted scarf in a way that turned it into a warm collar. Then he held her coat open while Olivia slipped first one arm and then the other into the sleeves. It was a courtesy he'd seen his father show his mother a hundred times but Heath only now realized it wasn't a favor, it was an act of love.

His heartbeat raced at the discovery.

"Thank you," she murmured over her shoulder as she wrestled with the zipper.

Heath was grateful that she couldn't see what might be showing on his face as the tender thought raced through his mind. How much of life had his selfish brain failed to process properly? What else would become clear if he saw more of the world through loving eyes?

"Let me grab my purse from upstairs."

"Don't be too long. I'm warming up the SUV."

When she was out of sight, Heath dropped down into the chair she'd vacated. He pressed his face into his palms and his mind cried out in the quiet place.

God, if You're listening, how about some help here! What am I supposed to do? I can't take back what's in the past. She'll never understand, never forgive that almost everything she believes about me is fake. Do I keep up with this farce and let her think she's loved by a jerk who just can't share her future because he's so wrapped up in his own life? Or is it better to keep my feelings to myself and not let Olivia know she's loved at all? How do I do the least damage?

Heath heard footsteps too heavy and slow to be Olivia's. He raised his face. Amos swore under his breath as he took the office side chair.

"Awww, I saw this coming," the old man

complained. "For her sake I'm askin' you to leave that girl alone. You cain't do anything but break Miss Livvy's heart and it may already be too late."

"Why are you so sure that's what'll happen?"

"Because when I look at you, it's like seein' myself in the mirror forty years ago. A leopard don't change his spots, boy. Not permanently. Oh, we may put others first for a time, but we always slide back into our selfish, pessimistic cocoons. And let's face it, we like it in that comfortable place because it's predictable and easy. If you don't get invested in other people you don't have to deal with their problems, put up with their mess."

There was no point in arguing with the truth. Amos's harsh words sank into Heath's gut like a punch to the belly. The honesty of it made Heath's stomach churn.

"Besides, she's out of your league." Amos let the final arrow fly.

Heels clicked as Olivia passed through the doorway.

"Okay, I'm ready for that doughnut. The Jack and Jill bakery is open late and they have espresso." Her voice was happy, excited.

She rubbed her hands together, anticipating the treat he'd offered. But now that Heath had been force-fed a load of guilt, he'd lost his appetite. As much as he hated to admit it, Amos was right.

Selfish was easy compared to the ache in Heath's chest that came from loving Olivia.

Chapter Seventeen

Olivia couldn't miss the fact that Heath's countenance had taken a downturn in the few minutes she'd been out of the room. When she stepped back into her cubicle she caught a sullen look that passed between the two men and wondered if something might have happened with Amos to make Heath reconsider his invitation.

"Have you changed your mind about going out?" she asked.

"Of course not." Heath came to his feet, seemed to shake off whatever was bugging him. He unlatched the front door and held it open. "After you."

"Don't forget about that favor I asked." Amos called out a reminder.

"Sure, whatever." Heath grumbled his response.

He took her hand, pulled her close to shield her

from the wind and helped her up into the Biddles'
big SUV. The interior was warm as toast because
of Heath's thoughtfulness.

"I can't believe they left this car for us to
use."

"They're special people. I've never known
anybody quite like them."

"The way y'all talk about one another, nobody
would guess you'd only met recently."

Heath trained his eyes on the road. "Do you
think some folks pass through our lives intentionally, even though it seems like a twist of fate?"

"Are we still talking about the Biddles?"

"Not so much. I was thinkin' more about you
and me. Do you believe it's by coincidence that
we met in this way and at this time?"

"Heath, God knew everything that would
happen in our lives before He knitted us together inside our mothers' bodies. He knew the
choices we'd have, the decisions we'd make and
the consequences we'd pay. He allowed us to
come into the world anyway, for better or worse.
Nothing happens by chance because God causes
all things to work together for those of us who
love Him."

She saw Heath smile in the soft red glow of
the dashboard dials. "You gave me another dose
before I even asked for it. That's second nature
to you, isn't it?"

She stuffed her gloved hands deeper into the pockets of her cozy winter coat.

"It hasn't always been that way," she admitted. "I was so angry with God a time or two that I wouldn't even speak with Him, much less live my life for Him."

"You're talking about losing your folks, right?"

"Yeah." Olivia wondered how much more she should say. This was not the conversation she'd intended to have during this short time together, but Heath was asking direct questions. She wanted to be honest and up-front about her past, just as he'd been.

"My mother's death and then my father's disappearance were each devastating in their own way. But then you add the public trashing of our name and my being ostracized by family members who were afraid of being associated with my lying thief of a father. The straw that broke the camel's back for me was the loss of my home. That'll make you pretty mad at the God of the universe who's supposed to love and provide for you. That's why I understand the anger my clients are feeling."

With his eyes still on the road ahead, Heath reached across the space between them to give a consoling touch to her wrist.

"How'd you get from all that anger to the peace you have today?"

Olivia slid her hand from her pocket and pressed it against Heath's upturned palm. He laced his fingers with hers, squeezing gently. She looked down at the place where they touched, then glanced up.

"I had to make a choice—run away from God and have no hope at all or trust Him completely and believe He would indeed be the Lord Who Provides. As He met all my needs, I began to serve others out of gratitude. That's when I learned what it meant to be His hands and feet in this world. And that's where He showed me He wanted me to feed the spiritual hunger of the people He put in my path as well as their physical hunger.

"There's peace to letting go of control and trusting God to work His plan out in your life. Any effort to struggle against His perfect will is about as rewarding as spitting into the wind."

"What a visual." Heath chuckled. His expression was part humor, part disgust. "I think maybe that's what I've been doing for years, spitting in the wind, thumbing my nose to the world and thinking the effort of one person couldn't make a permanent difference."

"Do you still feel that way?"

Heath was quiet for the time it took him to

park the vehicle in the bakery's mostly empty lot. He turned off the headlights, removed the key from the ignition and twisted to face her.

"Do I still feel one person can't make any difference?" He repeated the question.

He scooped her left hand between both of his and patted lightly, while he seemed to search for the answer.

"Olivia, for years I've viewed my work effort as a plug in a deep, old rain barrel that's full of holes and about to burst at the seams. The water level in the barrel rises as it rains day after day. The plugs leak or pop from the pressure, the water squirts out and more pours in from the top. Thinking like that made me complacent. I started to ask myself 'Why bother?'"

"So it was boredom with your work that made you take that foolish bet, huh? That's why you came over here and hacked into the city computer system?"

He grimaced, as if a troublesome thought had struck him. "Don't get me sidetracked from your first question, because I want you to hear my answer."

"Sorry," she apologized. He was so intent on continuing the thread of this conversation she almost wished she hadn't asked. Olivia had more she wanted to say to Heath before their hour got away from them.

"The long and short of it is that the sting of one fire ant can do some damage before you can squash it. But when every ant in the colony gets the notion to move in the same direction, they can take over Texas and there's not much can stop them."

Olivia squinted beautiful eyes and tilted her head to one side like a kitten trying to make sense out of its reflection in a mirror. Confusion made her even more adorable. Heath was just about desperate to pull her into his arms and tell her he loved her, but Amos's words were fresh in his mind.

"We may put others first for a time, but we always slide back into our selfish, pessimistic cocoons."

The old man came by his opinion through a lifetime of experience. If he was right, it wouldn't be long before Heath turned inward on himself again, forgetting how this moment felt. Olivia had come a long way, all by herself. She ought to have better than another dishonest, self-centered man in her life.

"Give me a second." She thumped her head with the heel of her free hand as if draining water from her ear, then grinned. "I thought I heard you say something about fire ants taking over Texas."

Heath grinned back. His metaphor hadn't made much sense.

"I'm doing a lousy job of saying what's in here." He tapped a finger against his chest.

Heath watched her smile slip away. Her face grew serious. He had to make her understand.

"Being around Table of Hope has shown me that one person's commitment can definitely have an impact. You've made things happen, you have the respect of your clients and your community. And now that you're going to get the chance to put your art out there, you have a barn burner of a future. You did that for yourself, Olivia. You proved to me that one person can make a difference. But you've always shown me that it's when God's people come together that the big jobs get done."

She lowered her chin, glanced down as if embarrassed.

"You're too kind, Heath."

"No, I'm not kind at all, and that's what I keep trying to tell you! Spending time with you has made me want to be a better man, to make a difference the way you have." He tugged at her hand, made her look into his face. "Listen, before we met I was ready to quit my job, move to the West Coast and start life over. I didn't think anybody would care because nothing I do seems to have a lasting impact. But I've decided I need to stay put, make a better effort at my job and toward the people affected by my work and my life."

"You're a very intense man, Heath. I can't imagine you ever giving anything less than your best. I'm sure your boss will be glad to have you back in Austin in a few more days."

Olivia's words were encouraging, but Heath heard sadness in her voice. Amos had been right to warn him off. She needed stability, honesty and trust in her life. And Heath needed to figure out how to have those for himself before he could ever hope to share them with another person. He owed it to the parents who loved him and the sisters who were searching for him to start the learning process with them.

The mood inside the truck was sinking so he bustled Olivia through the freezing parking lot and into the sweetly steamy interior of the bakery. He paid for their espresso double shots, a half-dozen glazed pastries and a sack of assorted rolls fresh from the oven. Then he took a chair across the small table from Olivia, sitting uncharacteristically with his back to the door.

"Oh, my goodness," she murmured a minute later over the rim of her cup. "This is divine." With eyes closed she popped the last bite of sausage kolache into her mouth and groaned appreciation.

"I thought you might like somebody else's coffee and sausage rolls before you got back into the kitchen tomorrow."

"Thank you for being so considerate." She wiped her fingers on a paper napkin, and then reached across the Formica surface to press her hand over his. He caught her fingertips and folded them protectively in his palm. "Heath, I need to tell you something while I have the chance and the courage."

"What could you possibly have to say that requires more than your usual nerves of steel?" he quipped, to lighten the solemn moment.

Olivia sat tall, tipped her eyes to the ceiling and pulled in a loud breath. She really did seem to be steadying herself. When her gaze met his again, it was as if her irises had expanded, the dark space of her eyes had grown from evening puddles to midnight pools.

"Heath, I've never known love, not romantic love anyway. I've read that it can take your breath away, make your heart race strangely and cause you to experience pleasure so intense that it's hardly bearable. Until a few days ago those sensations were for other people, not for me."

His heart thudded, beating an erratic rhythm. She was describing the crazy stuff he was feeling. Thank God it was happening to Olivia, too!

She leaned in and put her weight on her

forearms. She moved her face so close he couldn't miss the fact that her thick, black lashes faded to charcoal gray on the tips. He wanted to press his lips to her soft eyelids, spread kisses over her cheeks and capture her mouth until she was breathless.

"I'm askin' you to leave that girl alone," Amos had nagged. *"A leopard don't change his spots."*

"Heath, I love you." She punctuated the confession by squeezing his hand so tightly his heart felt the pressure. He willed himself to use his cop's instincts; sit tight, don't react.

When he didn't respond, heavy tears welled in her eyes. She blinked to keep them from falling.

"It's okay if you don't feel the same way. I just needed to get the words out before it was too late and I never got another chance."

I can't let Olivia say anything more. I can't let her speak words she'll regret when I'm gone.

He yanked her closer, planted an almost-desperate kiss against her mouth, then released her hands and fell away to press his spine to the plastic chair.

"I'm sorry. I shouldn't have done that," Heath said, apologizing for the actions even he didn't understand. He was over his head and out of his league, just as Amos had said. The thought chilled his very soul just as a cold blast of air from an open door sent a shiver down the back of his neck.

"Good evening, Officer!" The lady behind the bakery's counter called to the new arrival. "The usual?"

"To go, Bernice. You're a keeper." The response came from a familiar male voice. Heavy footsteps moved close. "Well, what a nice surprise on a crummy night."

Olivia raised her head, a forced smile replacing the shock that had been in her eyes moments earlier.

"Hey, Freddy." She nodded.

The tall cop stepped into Heath's field of vision, towering over the table. Weatherford took the hand Olivia extended and held on long enough to prove Heath's point.

"I didn't see your red truck outside."

"I'm here with a friend." She indicated Heath.

He pushed his chair back and stood, eyeball-to-eyeball. Man-to-man.

"Heath Stone," was all he offered, along with the required handshake.

"Have we met?" Weatherford asked.

"Not so you'd remember," Heath mumbled and took his seat again.

"Heath was helping me with errands the other day when you gave my truck a push."

The cop nodded, satisfied for the moment. "Everything going okay at your place?" he asked, dismissing Heath and focusing on Olivia.

"We've had some cases of the flu on our staff, like everybody else in Waco, but I think we'll be fine now that we've got some additional volunteers."

"Your order's ready," Bernice interrupted.

Weatherford opened his wallet and handed Olivia a business card. "Listen, if you need anything at all, you can call me at that number, day or night. I'll be glad to help out any way I can."

The headlights of the cruiser outside flashed impatiently.

"Duty calls," the officer explained to Olivia. With a jerk of his chin toward Heath, Weatherford traded cash for the carryout sacks and cups and headed for the door.

"Now do you see what I mean?" Heath stirred his coffee, kept his head down. "He's the buzzard, you're the bunny."

She took a sip of espresso and didn't acknowledge the comment he had no right to make. That was only fair, since he hadn't acknowledged the declaration of love he had no right to hear.

Chapter Eighteen

The next morning Olivia sat in her cubicle of an office and kept an eye on the front door. Her nerves were frayed rope, her stomach an angry beehive. If only Freddy hadn't interrupted her conversation with Heath last night, things might not have ended on such a strange note. Even so, she'd expected anything other than the silent treatment she got on the drive home.

Maybe she'd gone too far, but Olivia would take up dippin' snuff before she'd feel guilty for being honest about the way she felt. This morning she'd had plenty of time alone to consider those feelings she'd just *had* to share. Feelings that were unfamiliar, feelings that hurt like the dickens when they were exposed.

But in fairness to Heath, Olivia had to admit this new pain was self-inflicted. She could have kept her mouth shut, but no… And what did she expect from a man who naturally looked for the dark lining in every silver cloud?

If she'd taken a little more time to think it over, Heath might be at her side instead of hiding behind his to-do list this morning. It would be nice to have him present since he'd set this whole thing with the gallery into motion. Instead, he'd made himself scarce after muttering that an independent businesswoman didn't need help from any man to sell herself.

Lance had phoned to say he was on his way. He'd be coming to the front door any minute and she intended to get this over with in a hurry, take him straight upstairs where her amateurish paintings dominated the walls. It would be a short visit as soon as he realized the glimmer of talent reflected in the one canvas he'd seen needed a lot of development before she'd be able to show, if ever.

She leaned back in her creaky desk chair and spoke to the ceiling. "Why did I let myself be fooled into thinking I was ready for this?"

"Because you *are* ready, honey." A comforting voice carried over the top of the partition.

"For real?" Olivia collapsed in a spineless heap against her secondhand desk.

Peggy's sneakers squeaked as they carried her into the office where she plopped down in the side chair.

"For real." Her round face bore a broad smile. Olivia was relieved that there was nothing patronizing in the older woman's eyes. Peggy had called Olivia's paintings *stunning*. "You're just a nervous mama who's afraid she might be the only person who thinks her baby is beautiful."

"People do occasionally have ugly babies, you know," Olivia reminded her new friend.

Peggy leaned forward and reached for Olivia's hand. The touch was soft and gentle in a way she hadn't known since her mother's death.

"Everything was fine last night. You were so confident when you showed me your stuff. What happened after we went home to cause you to doubt yourself?"

Olivia's chin dipped toward her chest. Accepting defeat wasn't part of who she was inside. But she'd figured out last night that going for it only felt exhilarating when the effort was successful. Not getting the desired response turned out to be a drag. God must intend for her to learn a lesson from this failure.

Lord, couldn't You wait a little while longer or take a different approach? Is it really necessary to make Your point with my very first love?

"Well?" Peggy prodded.

"Remember how you asked me yesterday if Heath knew that I care for him?"

Peggy nodded and scooted closer for the details.

"I took that chance last night and it didn't work out so well." Olivia kept her voice low.

"What?" Peggy's one-word question was a shriek of disbelief.

"We went out for a while and I took advantage of the time alone to tell Heath how I feel about him."

"And his reaction?"

Olivia sighed, felt her face growing warm with embarrassment. "At first he just sat there like a bump on a log."

"Did he come right out and say he didn't feel the same way?"

"He didn't need to say anything. I could tell by the look on his face—he was mortified. Then he gave me a quick little pity kiss and he even apologized for doing that."

Peggy's expression morphed from disbelief to sympathy.

"Oh, honey. If I'd kept my thoughts to myself, you wouldn't be in this awkward spot right now."

"It's not your fault, Peggy. I'm a big girl and I knew I was taking a risk."

"But I feel awful, as if I set you up to get hurt."

Olivia fanned away Peggy's remorse. There was no point in both of them feeling foolish.

"Is there anything I can do to help fix things?"

"Stick close for a couple of days and that might keep me from shoving even more of my big foot into my mouth. By then he'll be back in Austin and I can nurse this battered pride that has no place in my life anyway."

"What if he's not? Back in Austin, I mean. Heath could hang around Waco, you know."

"Listen to me." Olivia shook her head at the notion. She had no idea where Peggy was going with this false encouragement. "That's not going to happen. Last night he admitted that being at Table of Hope has helped change his attitude about work. Instead of running off to a new job in another city he's going to stay where he is and rededicate himself to his career. He wants to have an impact, make a difference. So, something positive has come of his community service after all and that'll just have to be enough for me."

Peggy seemed accepting, almost pleased by the news.

"In that case it'll be an honor to be your Girl Friday for as long as you need me," she agreed.

The buzzer jolted both women out of their

confidential moment. Somebody was at the entrance.

"That'll be Lance."

Olivia stood, shot the cuffs of her only dress blouse out the sleeves of her least worn-out sweater and brushed down the front of her jeans, wishing for the first time ever that she owned a pair of tailored wool slacks.

"You're a class act no matter what you're wearing." Peggy sensed Olivia's discomfort with the way she looked. "And your paintings are incredible. Don't be nervous."

Olivia crossed the short length of her office and stopped just inside the cubical doorway. Pretending to take something off her head, she perched it on the coat rack and then settled another invisible hat, adjusted it just so and then checked her image reflected by the wall mirror.

"What are you doing?" Peggy chuckled at the make-believe behavior.

"I thought it might help if I took off my business owner's hat and put on my artist's hat for this meeting. Then as soon as this is over I'll need to switch to my Pilgrim hat so we can start getting ready for our Thanksgiving feast."

"There must be a ton of work involved in preparing a meal for so many people."

"You got that right," Olivia warned. "It'll definitely keep me distracted from personal matters for a while."

At least I hope so.

Heath was in a sorry mood, made worse by the fact that it was his own fault.

Olivia and that guy from Studio Gallery had been in her apartment for over an hour. Heath was about to make an excuse to find out for himself what was going on up there. He'd adjusted every hinge on every door while waiting on the people overhead to reappear and he was running out of excuses for hanging out at the bottom of Olivia's stairwell.

Amos was keeping an eye on him and Heath knew it. The old guy had been scowling all morning, but with such a sourpuss, how could a body tell when the man was skulking about for a reason or just being his miserably normal self? He'd made his point and there was no need to keep driving it home with piercing looks and disapproving grunts.

Feet thumped in the stairwell, excited voices floated down the steps, and the door flung wide with one easy touch, thanks to the overdose of WD-40 Heath had applied.

He caught sight of Biddle's wife.

"Oh, Heath! I'm glad to find you out here."

Her greeting was overly enthusiastic, friendly to the point of being suspicious.

The owner of the gallery appeared, looking as pleased as a huntin' dog on the first day of squirrel season. Olivia was last, pushing the door closed behind her. When she turned toward the others her eyes grazed Heath's momentarily and then she returned her attention to her visitor.

"Lance, you remember Heath, of course." Olivia acknowledged him. How nice of her.

"Good to see you again, Stone."

Heath held up the spray can of lubricant and a red rag to deflect the obligatory handshake.

"You were right about Miss Wyatt's talent. It's unique, very exciting." He smiled at Olivia. "We're going to work well together."

The man who'd been so professional at the gallery was all but salivating over Olivia today. The thought of escorting him off the property was tempting.

The few hours Heath had spent on the narrow bunk last night had been nearly sleepless. His chest ached from the shuddering and shivering of a tender heart that had barely existed a week ago. He'd groaned, grieved and given God a fit over Olivia's confession of love. If she'd never blurted out how she felt, then things would still be going according to plan. But he'd not only heard those precious words from the lips he found so appealing, he'd memorized her statement and now he could repeat it over and over and over again.

He could kick himself for that hasty excuse of a kiss. Amos was right, it was inevitable; Heath would spoil everything eventually. The same sullen ways that had kept him from being close to his parents would be a roadblock keeping Olivia at a distance. It would never come naturally to put another person's happiness first, thanks to the self-centered thinking that kept him alive on the job.

And speaking of the job, he'd begun to see it as his mission field, a dangerous place to find out if he really might make a difference. Heath hadn't been willing to put his parents or the sisters he'd never met at risk so he certainly wouldn't expose Olivia. If he stayed undercover, he'd never have the family he'd come to want with all his soul.

He mentally complained about his circumstances.

If I hadn't been sent on this assignment barefaced, this might be a whole different story. But instead—

"Heath." Olivia interrupted the roller coaster of thought that was derailing his life. "We're headed to the big room to sit down and review the gallery's standard contract."

"And you want me to look over it with you?" At least she still valued his opinion.

"Actually, I asked Peggy to help with the legal stuff." Olivia offered him a weak smile. "Since you didn't set up the coffee stations today I was hoping that maybe you could put the kettle on and bring us some hot tea."

"Sure thing, *Miss Livvy.*" Heath complied, as if he had a choice.

Man! I am such a loser.

Peggy Biddle snickered.

He trailed along behind the small group and peeled off into the kitchen when they kept going. He set up the tray exactly as he'd seen Olivia do it, filling the ceramic pot and covering it with the cozy thing she claimed kept it warm. He fished around in the pantry for some of her fancy herbal tea bags, dumped a pack of Fig Newtons on an extra saucer for something sweet and took a moment to admire his work. English High Tea if there ever was one. His mama would be so proud.

He stopped at the door to the big room, inhaled deeply of the same air Olivia was breathing. It was scented with homemade biscuits and Pine-Sol; two things that represented her gifts of service. She had done incredible work in this place and deserved all the support she could get from him, starting right now. If this was what she needed, then by golly he'd put a smile on his face and serve the lady a cup of tea.

"So if you'll sign right there, I'll arrange for our driver to pick up your canvases this afternoon. We'll kick off your show with a catered meet-and-greet on Saturday evening."

"This Saturday?" Olivia squeaked.

Lance smiled, seemed unconcerned about moving so fast. "Yes, ma'am. The holidays are perfect for launching a new artist. I can get the promotion running on our site tomorrow morning and I'll send an online invitation out to our best clients by noon."

"Beg pardon." Heath elbowed his way into the center of the discussion. "Hot tea, as ordered." He set the tray before Olivia. She looked up, mouthed her thanks and caught the cue Heath was sending by cutting his eyes toward the door.

"Excuse me for a moment, please." She pushed her chair away, stood and headed for the hallway. "Peggy, would you mind pouring while I run and get some milk?"

"My bad—forgot the milk." Heath shrugged and followed her to the kitchen.

"What is it?" She didn't seem pleased.

"I want to know what he offered you."

Olivia rolled her eyes, definitely not happy. She snatched a carton from the cooler and filled a small pitcher.

"This is none of your business and what would you know about working with a gallery anyway?"

"Password-protecting your computers can't keep me off those old machines," Heath informed her.

"What's that got to do with anything?" She planted a fist on each hip.

"I was online most of the night figuring out how this contract with an art gallery works. You ought to have the last say on pricing the paintings and the artist always gets the highest percentage of the profits. So don't let old Lance make you think that just because this is your first rodeo, you don't know a longhorn from a buffalo."

That expression Heath couldn't decipher settled over Olivia's face. Her eyes held no sparkle and her pupils became pinpoints of dark heat burning holes in his intentions. Her full lips compressed into a bout of disapproval.

"For the life of me I don't know why you care, Heath. Your time here is technically over since you've been on duty around the clock. Your sentence is served and Detective Biddle can vouch for your work. You don't even need my signature on your release form, so you can leave anytime you're ready."

Heath was stunned by the lack of emotion in Olivia's voice. If her feelings could transition to apathy in twelve hours, how much truth was there to her profession of love?

Yeah, like I've got the right to question her honesty, huh, God?

"Is that what you want?" Heath asked. *Please say no.*

"What I want is for you to pray about this and listen for the guidance of the Holy Spirit. Then do what you feel in your heart is right, even if it's only right for you, Heath. I'll be okay. This may be my first rodeo, as you put it, but I've been around the backside of a horse enough to recognize one when I see it."

The echo of a buzzer announced a visitor at the front entry. Olivia looked toward the sound, and then down at the carton of milk she still held in her hand.

"I don't think Amos is out there right now."

"I'll see who that is," Heath offered. "You go back and wrap up your deal. You're right, this is none of my business and I should get out of your hair sooner rather than later." He turned around and marched down the long hallway that led to the check-in area. Outside the door, with burglar bars and glass to keep him away from Olivia stood the person who was quite possibly responsible for this whole mess.

Dick Sheehan.

Chapter Nineteen

Olivia's heart had been on a wild ride all day. One moment it was in the pit of her stomach as she waited for Heath to pack his few belongings and leave. And an hour later the erratic thumping had climbed into her throat, thanks to Heath digging in his heels as if he were there for the long haul.

"I said I'd stay through Thanksgiving and I'm staying through Thanksgiving," he insisted when she found him in the kitchen making a mess with a potato peeler. Bits of sweet potato skin littered the countertop, floor and wall behind him while Heath clutched a mutilated yam as if it might try to make an escape.

"He's determined to help out in here," Amos explained. "With a hundred pounds of taters to peel, I figured I'd best put both of these guys to work."

Olivia noticed Dick Sheehan for the first time.

"Welcome back! I didn't realize you were in here."

"Word's out that Table of Hope will be open again tomorrow. I figured you might need some help with the holiday coming up and all," Sheehan explained.

"That's thoughtful of you. Thanks so much for showing up like this."

She was always glad for another willing worker, especially a guy who already knew his way around the shelter.

"I let him in a while ago," Heath grumbled, sounding for all the world like Amos.

"My pleasure, Miss Livvy." Dick held up his half-peeled sweet potato. "Don't these things come already sliced and in cans? Wouldn't that be easier on the kitchen staff?"

Heath and Amos exchanged withering glances.

"You gonna take it or you want me to?" Heath gave Amos first dibs.

"Go ahead." Amos turned his attention to the tub of turkeys he was injecting with Cajun marinade.

"Money doesn't grow on trees around here." Heath parroted what he'd heard Amos say a few days earlier. "In case you hadn't noticed, we work with whatever gets donated."

Olivia held back a grin. *My, how Heath's perspective has changed since his first KP experience.*

"Excuse me." Dick exaggerated an apology, and then turned his attention back to Olivia. "You think I could bunk here tonight since the place is empty?"

"I can't imagine why not."

"Don't you need clearance from the Health Department or something?" Heath barked above the manic scraping of his peeler.

"We didn't get shut down for goodness' sake— we closed voluntarily." Olivia wanted to knock a knot on Heath's head for the unnecessary comment.

"Still, flu bugs and all," he grumbled. "Might not be smart to let just anybody back in here too soon."

"Could I speak with you for a moment in my office?" She turned and strode toward her cubicle, expecting Heath to follow.

"What is going on with you?" She flew hot the moment he stepped into her workspace. "First you're hiding out, then you're all up in my business, next you're leaving and now you're staying. Not only that, you're trying to run off what little help we have."

"I don't think I like that guy."

"I don't care what you think!"

"Well, you should. He looks suspicious and I wouldn't trust him any further than I could drop-kick him."

Olivia huffed out a breath at the judgmental comment.

"Dick's a homeless man who's willing to work in exchange for a place to sleep tonight. In case you've forgotten, Heath, this is a shelter and I don't turn people away because of how they look, or whether or not they seem trustworthy. I let *you* in, didn't I?" The wisecrack slipped out, surprising even Olivia.

Heath grabbed the stapler from her desk and held it like a microphone to his mouth. "Sarcastic party of one, your table is ready."

Olivia spit out a grin. She'd come to enjoy his edgy humor. Even so, he had no right to be critical of her clients. He folded his arms, evidently waiting for the lecture he knew he had coming.

"Look, Dick was a good sport when the other guys were sick and you needed somebody to help you clean up the mess. I'm asking you to give him the benefit of the doubt and just appreciate his servant's heart."

Heath became interested in the pattern of the area rug. He nodded while he muttered something she couldn't understand, which was probably just as well.

"I'll take that as a sign of agreement."

His gaze wandered up to meet hers, his eyes staring, questioning. "I don't know what to take as a sign anymore."

Olivia stepped closer, nearly toe-to-toe with Heath. She raised her hand, rested her palm along his jaw and studied the face that had begun to appear in her dreams and daydreams.

"I'm sorry," she whispered.

"For what?"

"For changing things between us, for making you uncomfortable, for saying something I should have kept to myself."

"But it's the truth, right?" he asked quietly.

"I've tried to be as honest with you as you've been with me."

Heath turned his face toward her hand, pressed his mouth to her palm and let his lips linger there for a moment. She felt the depth of his warm sigh against her fingertips. Then he took a step back as if he were creating a chasm between them.

"It's good of you to stay through the holiday," she thanked him. "I appreciate it." What more could she say?

Heath seemed uncomfortable with her gratitude and let his attention shift to the window. He stepped closer, breathed against the glass and touched the foggy spot that appeared.

"With this ice storm passing across the state, it's a good thing you're opening the doors again tomorrow. The forecast says it's going to be the worst Thanksgiving cold spell on record."

"Well, let's pray the weatherman is wrong."

"Why's that?" Heath turned to face her.

"Because when it freezes in a place like Waco, where we're not used to such cold, people on the street die."

Heath hoped Olivia's comment wasn't a premonition. A drug bust could be deadly business. If things went according to plan, they'd be drawing the pill pushers to a new location on the very night the freeze was supposed to hit the lowest temps. Who knew if the bait Amos had thrown into uncertain waters would get a bite right away. But if Heath's suspicions were correct, the sellers were greedy for a cash deal, anxious to unload a huge quantity and then hightail it out of the state as quickly as possible.

"So, will you make nice with the help?" Olivia's head was cocked to one side. Her short black hair poked out every which way, a sign she'd nervously run her hands through it, which he'd noticed she did frequently.

"For you, anything." He meant it from the heart, wished he could prove it to her.

"Yeah, thanks a lot." Her gratitude was anemic. She left the room and headed down the hallway. "I really appreciate your support."

Olivia's words dripped insincerity. Heath took a beat to consider how much that bothered him. He'd been saying that she *should* be suspicious, question more than she accepted. She needed to expect the worst from people so she couldn't be taken for a ride. That's the perspective Olivia ought to have after the hard knocks in her life, but instead she was one of those cockeyed optimists, too good to be true. Heath's insides shivered. The power behind her positive nature had become clearer to him by the day and he no longer felt the need to deny the source.

Heath was alone in the quiet space. Alone in the world for that matter. He hung his head.

"Lord, Olivia says You're in control and You can do anything. Whatever Your plan is for the next few days, when it's all played out will You please help me learn to be less of a jerk? I want to be a person my family will be proud to claim, I want to be a cop who doesn't have to be afraid to show his face. I want to be a man who deserves a woman's love. That's pretty much a new person, and Olivia says that's exactly the business You're in. How 'bout it, God?"

"Stone, you down there?" Amos interrupted Heath's pitiful effort at prayer. A raspy cough punctuated the question.

Heath poked his head outside Olivia's cubicle, motioned silently to Amos. The older man entered the check-in area and pulled the hall door closed behind him, then followed Heath into the private space.

"I don't think Sheehan's our guy." Amos wiped at his face with a checkered handkerchief.

"Why do you say that?"

"He's too stupid."

"I won't disagree, but could you be more specific?"

"I dropped a couple of hints when we were alone in the kitchen. Stuff any seasoned doper would pick up on. He was more concerned about how many sweet potatoes were in that bushel basket than where a fella could score something big for a holiday party."

Heath slumped against the wall, back to square one.

"I never thought it was him anyway." Amos struggled through another fit of coughing that drained the color from his weathered face.

"Are you sure you feel like being up and about just yet? Maybe you should take it easy for a while longer."

"I'll be fine." Amos dismissed the concern as he stuffed the handkerchief in his hip pocket. "Croupy lungs are what I deserve for smokin' two packs a day for twenty years."

"Okay, what were you saying about not suspecting Sheehan all along?"

"Mostly gut feeling, but he's only been coming around here for a few weeks. This surge of campus drugs has been steady for a while now."

"How would you know about that?"

Amos slanted an impatient glance at Heath. "I may look like a washed-up old coot on the outside but that's not how I feel in here." He pressed a gnarled hand to his chest. "I have a lifetime of experience as a cop and a family man. The bad times didn't always outweigh the good ones and I didn't drink so much that it pickled my memory."

"Sorry, I didn't mean to imply—"

"Yes, ya did. You don't expect a has-been like me to be in touch with what's going on in my community, but I am. I read the paper, listen to the news and pay attention to talk inside the shelter. Anybody who's really interested can figure out that we're smack in the middle of a drug traffic lane and kids are gonna die if it's not stopped." The outburst cost Amos another coughing fit. Heath grabbed an unopened bottle of water from Olivia's desk, twisted the cap and handed it to Amos. He drank to clear and calm his throat.

"Thanks," he wheezed.

"Don't mention it."

"Not the water," Amos clarified. "I mean

thanks for looking out for Miss Livvy. She thinks she's got it all under control. She's mighty sharp—I'll give her that—but she needs help. For Pete's sake, she's only a kid."

"She's not much younger than me."

Amos rolled his eyes. "You came into the world a grumpy old man. You started life thinkin' the worst of folks, and thanks to your line of work now you expect it. Miss Livvy's not jaded like you and me. She can still be happy as long as she gets the chance." He punctuated the remark with a glare of overkill. "And while I've got the chance I want to thank you for protecting her and keeping this place in the clear. As soon as you make tracks in another direction, she can get on with the stuff she's got planned for Table of Hope."

"What about her art? Will you encourage her?"

"How about if we both just let go and let God handle it?"

The buzzer sounded, giving them both a start.

"What the…" Amos bit back his thought. They looked around the cubicle wall to find several bundled up figures stamping their feet to keep warm on the porch. "Looks like we might be back in business sooner than we expected."

When the bolt was turned, the door flung wide

and scarves unwound, revealing Bruce, Nick and Velma looking much better than the last time Heath had laid eyes on the three of them.

"The fever and chills are all gone," Velma reported.

"And no barfing since we left here," Bruce added.

"Let's hope that's not a commentary on the food, considering you're second in command in the kitchen." Amos pulled Bruce into a bear hug, the two men slapping each other on the back, careful not to set off coughing spells. "You sure you're not out of bed too soon?"

Bruce shook his head. "Even though the nurses treated us like royalty, we couldn't wait to be released. The minute we got the all clear we were dressed and out the door. We just happened to hitch a ride with the same van that was picking up Velma."

"Y'all think you're in good enough shape to help with Thanksgiving?" Amos still seemed worried about his friends.

"By the grace of God!" they chorused.

"Then I can't wait for the look on Miss Livvy's face when she sees we're all back together." Amos led the way. "And guess what? Our girl is gonna have an art show at a real gallery."

The four trooped down the hall, communing in friendship, gone in search of their boss lady.

Heath watched them go, leaving him behind with his thoughts. Her staff was back and with Peggy still there Olivia had all the help she needed. Tomorrow would be a big day one way or the other and then Heath could be free to "make tracks in another direction" as Amos had put it.

Everything was falling right into place. Here was another of those *signs* he'd just told Olivia he didn't know how to interpret. But this one was so obvious even he couldn't deny the message. His prayer for help was still fresh on his lips and here was a response. He reached into his pocket where his fingers grazed the warm metal of his cell phone.

Olivia was busy reconnecting with the people who were her family. It was time for Heath to do the same. He punched the first speed-dial number, excited to hear the voice that answered.

"Mom, it's me. I called to see what you and Dad are doing for Thanksgiving. I sure could use one of your home-cooked meals. And we'll need extra in case I'm able to convince company to join us."

Chapter Twenty

It was two days before her very first Thanksgiving at Table of Hope and Olivia's heart was full to overflowing with emotion.

Tonight she was surrounded by friends. Tomorrow they'd help prepare the huge holiday meal and then welcome returning clients in the afternoon. Thursday her new family would spend Thanksgiving together, and then on Friday she'd concentrate on learning something about each interior decorator and art collector on the list Lance had provided. It was unbelievable, but on Saturday she would be the guest of honor at Studio Gallery, making her debut as a local artist.

Father, forgive me. This shower of blessings should be plenty for anyone, but a busy schedule isn't enough to crowd thoughts of Heath from my mind. He'll be gone before I know it and my first touch of love will be nothing more than a scar on my heart. Help me to let go of myself while we worship tonight, Lord. Let it be all about You and nothing about me.

"I knew it!" Velma was triumphant.

Olivia raised her eyes from the well-worn Bible open on her lap. Velma had plopped front and center into the row of chairs set up for study. Her eyes were clear of fever and sparkling once again with the pure mischief Olivia had come to love in her friend.

"Knew what?" She was almost afraid to find out.

"You got it goin' on with that good lookin' fella."

"I don't have anything *goin' on,* period."

"Oh, please, girl. I'd have to be one of the three blind mice to miss the way he looks at you."

Olivia's insides quaked. "And just what is it you've noticed?"

"Since you're shamelessly asking, I'm gonna tell ya." Velma's grin spread wider and she slid her chair close.

"That man would hardly raise his head from his plate a few days ago for fear somebody might look him in the eye. But if you asked him what we had for dinner tonight, I doubt he could say. He was watching you and brooding like a love-struck teen. And you weren't much better."

Velma was right. As glad as Olivia was to focus on her friends and catch up on the past few days, her attention kept straying to Heath. It would have been easier to stop drawing breath than to ignore him at her table. Each time their eyes locked, it was like their hands touching, their spirits embracing.

Heath loves me.

Olivia was certain of it, knew it as sure as she knew the sun would come up in the morning. Whatever fueled his reluctance to admit his feelings was just as strong as the excitement that had forced her to tell him how she felt. But nothing was more powerful than the God she served and Olivia trusted His plan more than she trusted human emotions. Still, the urge to fight this battle on her own was almost overwhelming.

"That obvious, huh?" Olivia acknowledged Velma's astuteness. Her hand settled on Olivia's knee to emphasize that something important was coming.

"There's no shame in it, Miss Livvy. So don't think you have to hide it under a bushel basket."

Olivia smiled. "That's exactly what Heath said to me about my painting."

"He's good lookin' *and* smart. You could do a whole lot worse."

The others began to find their seats so Velma scooted her chair away and took up her Bible. Peggy and Mary Sue claimed the seats beside Velma. Heath sat on the end, arms folded across his chest. His body language still said he was closed off, but Olivia knew better.

She opened their time together with a prayer of thanks and then moved straight into the story of Jonah and his call to preach repentance to the seafaring city of Nineveh.

"Most everybody knows the action-adventure part of the story. Jonah ran away from God's command and boarded a ship headed in the opposite direction. During a storm he was thrown overboard by the crew, but God saved Jonah's life by sending a great fish to swallow him whole. Inside the belly of the fish he spent three days and nights crying out to God and in His mercy God commanded the fish to spit Jonah out on dry land."

"I can sure relate to having something in your belly that wants out!" Bruce teased.

"Please." Heath blocked the very thought by covering his ears with both hands. "No reminders. Those were the grossest few days of my life."

"We'd have been in a world of hurt if you hadn't come along when you did and been willing to do the dirty work," Amos admitted.

"Yeah, thanks, man," Bruce added. Nick nodded, too.

"Trust me, if I'd known community service was gonna involve helping you guys in and out of the shower, I'd have opted for thirty days in the hole."

The men shared companionable laughter, obviously bonded through the dire circumstances.

"And speaking of community service—" Olivia winked at the ladies as she wrestled the men's attention back to their study. "What Jonah did for Nineveh is the part of this story we might not remember because we get stuck on the amazing transportation God used to deliver His messenger." She waited for more snickers.

"The message is always the most important part and in this case it saved a population almost exactly the same size as Waco."

"For real?" Nick asked.

"The Scripture calls Nineveh a great city of over 120,000 people. God planned to destroy them all."

"So, Jonah's visit was that important?"

"It wasn't Jonah's visit, Nick. It was his obedience. The ironic thing is the people of Nineveh respected God—they just wouldn't obey Him."

Amos joined in the explanation. "They were too big for their britches, thinkin' they could behave any which way and get away with it. The

Lord gives us a lot of rope and the free will to decide what to do with it. If we're smart, we tie one end to Him and hang on to the other for dear life. If we're too smart for our own good we wrap that rope around our necks and jump off a cliff. Those are the times when we find out that if our anchor isn't Jesus Christ we're just free-fallin' fools." Amos looked a little embarrassed. "Sorry for taking over, Miss Livvy, but I've been there and done that. These young folks can learn something from an old man if they'll just have some respect for the voice of experience."

"Amos is right," Peggy added. "We choose our paths every day and we have only ourselves to blame when things go wrong. Eventually, God gets fed up. The Ninevites were so filled with wickedness, He decided to destroy them. But first He gave them one last chance."

"By sending Jonah, you mean?" Nick was engrossed in the story.

"Exactly." Olivia prepared to wrap up the lesson. "Jonah preached and warned that they had forty days to repent and then their city would be decimated. Everyone, from the king right down to the last dock worker knew Jehova God meant business. They put on itchy sackcloth, went without food and spent all their time praying for God to change His mind. Velma, would you read Jonah 3:10 for us, please?"

"When God saw what they did and how they turned from their evil ways, He had compassion and did not bring upon them the destruction He had threatened."

"But those were Old Testament times. God doesn't destroy whole cities like that anymore."

"Nick, God can do anything He wants to do." Every eye in the room was on Heath as he spoke. "His authority hasn't diminished since the days of Jonah. And neither has His ability to forgive people who change their ways."

Silence hung in the room as if everyone held their breath.

"Heath's right," Olivia agreed. "God asks for repentance and obedience and in return He shows compassion."

"And then everything's okay?" Nick's voice was hopeful.

"You know better than that." Heath spoke up again. "I'm sure there was still plenty of suffering in Nineveh to go around, but God did spare their lives. Even though He's the God of second chances, it's up to us to do things right after He forgives us. And even with forgiveness there are still consequences. Sooner or later bad choices catch up with everybody."

Olivia's ribs ached from the frantic pounding of her heart beneath her sweater. Heath really did get what his parents had tried to give him all those years ago. The Word was down deep inside him and it just needed God's perfect timing to rise up out of his spirit.

Thank You, Father!

Heath worried that he'd said too much. Where did he get off adding his two cents, as if anybody cared? It wasn't his place to speak up during Olivia's teaching. Still, there was a sweet look of peace on her beautiful face, as if she was glad for his participation.

"Thank you, Miss Livvy," Nick spoke up.

His face had gone so white Heath thought the boy might pass out.

"That's what I needed to hear tonight. I've missed everyone—" Nick's voice broke away. He nearly choked on his words.

Olivia nodded at Bruce, who said the closing prayer and then suggested they meet in the kitchen so he could hand out tomorrow's assignments.

Heath hung back, watched as Amos slipped a grandfatherly arm over Nick's shoulder and guided him away from the big room.

Peggy waved goodbye, promising to be back with the sunrise.

When they were alone, Heath apologized. Sorta.

"I can't seem to stop pokin' my nose into your business."

"Making disciples is everybody's business. It was cool to see you making it yours, too."

"So, what I said was okay?"

"It was perfect. Solomon wrote that when parents train their children correctly, they'll remember their faith when they're grown. I'd say your folks deserve a pat on the back for a job well done."

Heath nodded. In a couple days he'd tell his mama face-to-face that she hadn't just been spinning her wheels after all.

"Your parents did well in other ways, too, Heath. I know you don't think of yourself as a gentleman, but that's what you've become."

His scalp prickled, as if the blood were quickly draining from his head and face. And from his heart. He was a snake, as cold-blooded, calculating and deceitful as the serpent in the Bible. When Olivia learned the truth, she'd want to crush his gentleman's ways beneath the heel of her boot.

"Why do you keep overlooking my flaws and giving me the benefit of the doubt? I don't deserve that," he insisted.

"Heath, you're the only one who's obsessing about your perceived faults, so they must bother you. If you don't intend to change those things, then concentrate on the positives in your life—"

He interrupted by taking hold of Olivia's wrists and pulling her close. He guided her hands up around his neck, released his grip and slipped his arms around her slender waist. She waited, dark eyes staring up into his face, unwilling to take the initiative this time.

"Olivia, you are the most amazing woman I've ever met, so that qualifies *you* as the positive thing in my life. If I concentrate on you for a moment, would you stop making excuses for me?"

"I'll do my best."

Heath saw the glimmer of a smile begin to curve her lips. When he covered her mouth with his the grin slipped away, a sigh resonated in her throat. He pressed her close, spreading his fingers wide across Olivia's slender back to pull her nearer.

Her hands were soft and warm on the back of his neck. He sizzled from her touch on his nearly shaved head to the tips of his toes, sensations he'd never expected to experience. She leaned into him, perfectly made for him in every way.

"Ahem." Amos fake coughed and knocked on the door.

Heath's arms slid away from her body as they moved apart. Olivia's face had never looked more beautiful, flushed pink as it was from their kiss. Her brows knitted and she pressed fingers to her lips, as if worried that she had only imagined the moment.

"I apologize for interrupting but most everybody's about to call it a day. Before I hit the hay I need a word with you, Heath. Then you can finish your *conversation* with Miss Livvy."

What Amos really meant was *once I've had my say you can get back to your monkey business if you dare*. Heath was no boy who deserved a trip to the woodshed. Even if he had been caught red-handed by the very person who expected the worst of him, he was still a grown man.

Olivia was very much a grown woman and they'd done nothing to be ashamed of.

Amos turned, stomped away. They stood still until the footsteps faded. Olivia's eyes were downcast. Was she disappointed that he'd kissed her or disappointed that the kiss had ended too soon?

"I think we'd better say goodnight." He touched her chin, raised it so her gaze met his.

"May I ask a big favor, Heath?"

"Name it."

"Would you please drive back over for my art gallery launch on Saturday? It would mean so much to have you there."

"It's a date."

Olivia nodded, and then wisely turned to leave the room. She slowed at the door, looked back. "I'll see you tomorrow, right?"

"Where else would I be?" he insisted, as if the question was absurd.

But if circumstances unfolded as expected, he might be called anywhere in the city in the next twenty-four hours. And after that he'd be back on his home turf, starting the new life his calls today had set into motion.

The oddest sensation thickened his throat and wouldn't be swallowed down. He held one arm outward, unable to miss the trembling in his hand. It was something he hadn't experienced in years.

Fear.

Not of a drug deal that might go wrong. Or of a family who wouldn't be patient with him while he became the man he wanted to be.

The fear was stronger than any he'd ever known.

Heath was afraid of losing Olivia.

Chapter Twenty-One

"Have you spoken to Heath today?" Olivia asked for the third time that morning since she'd come downstairs. Nobody had talked to him. Nobody had even seen him since their Bible study the night before.

Amos shuffled across the kitchen floor with a heavy tray of candied yams. He eased it into one of the wall-mounted ovens and then double-checked the temperature before turning to face her.

"Can't say as I have," he answered her question as he wiped his hands on the skirt of his apron.

"You two didn't exchange cross words last night, did you?"

"What would make you suspect such a thing?" Amos was brimming with more sarcasm than usual.

Olivia mentally counted to ten when what she

really wanted to do was bounce him out if he'd been meddling. But Amos was like a grandfather, so it was natural that he'd turn a critical eye on any man who showed her attention.

Not that there had been such a man before or might ever be again!

"Amos, I know you don't approve of what you saw last night."

He scowled and growled, a toothless old papa bear still defending his grown cub.

She moved close, wrapped him in a hug. She patted his back, feeling how much thinner he was since his bout with flu.

"I'm twenty-seven years old. You don't want me to be alone forever, do you?"

"Of course not," he muttered near her ear and then leaned back to look into her face. "But kissin' that toad won't make him turn into Prince Charming."

She smiled at Amos, gave his shoulders a playful shake. "Heath will be gone in a day or two, so where's the harm?"

"Right there." Amos tapped his index finger just below her left collarbone. "I'm afraid the harm's already been done. I just hope it's not permanent."

"I love him, Amos." The quiet admission burst out.

"Oh, good gravy. You don't know anything

about the guy." Amos's whiskered jaw sagged, his arms fell away as if they were suddenly made of petrified wood.

"I know more than you probably think, and it's enough for me."

Amos shook his head and moved behind the prep counter.

"Heath's an honorable man with values and morals. You said yourself—we'd have been up a creek without him."

"Yeah, well, now your heart will be up a creek because of him and I don't like that one bit."

Olivia was about to give up on the conversation. She'd already said too much and it hadn't accomplished a thing, apart from upsetting Amos. She needed to find Heath.

"So, did you and Heath have words last night or not?"

"Not. Nick needed some advice and I thought having an opinion from a man closer to his own age might help. Last time I saw the two of them they'd stepped outside to talk privately."

"Thanks, I'll see what Nick can tell me."

"Nick's gone back to Waco General at least for the day."

"What? Why don't I know anything about this?"

"I'm sure you noticed he was green around the gills after supper. Peggy took one look at him this morning and drove him right back over to the hospital to sleep it off there. Said she wasn't having anybody sick in the same building where she was making forty dozen biscuits and five gallons of giblet gravy."

"That's certainly understandable, but I wish somebody would clue me in on this stuff beforehand."

"You've got your own to-do list to worry about and everything's under control in the kitchen. We'll be okay without Nick since Peggy and her husband are both here today."

"Where do you want this?" Detective Biddle stood in the doorway with a fifty-pound sack of flour hoisted on his shoulder.

"In that far corner," Peggy instructed from right behind him. "Set it inside that galvanized tub so I can get to it as I need it."

"Good morning, you two. Sorry I'm so late coming downstairs." Olivia's guilt meter was in the red zone. She'd spent entirely too much time on the phone with Lance, answering his questions about her paintings. He was putting a brochure together and with time so compressed between the holiday and the meet-and-greet he had to get the information right away. "I should have my head examined for taking on something else this weekend."

"That's nonsense," Peggy disagreed. "The

timing couldn't be more perfect and God dropped it right into your lap by using Heath the way He did to introduce you to that gallery owner."

"Speaking of Heath, nobody's seen him since last evening and I'm kind of worried. Could he get into trouble for being missing in action today?" Olivia looked to Biddle for an answer.

"You said he's been working around the clock, right?

"Yep, puts in twenty-hour days," Amos spoke up.

"Then his obligation has been more than fulfilled and he's free to return to Austin."

"Since it's a holiday week, maybe he had plans," Peggy chimed in.

"That's my guess. I bet his mama's cookin' a big Thanksgiving dinner for their family. We really don't know that much about him." Amos's unnecessary words stung, but there was truth in what he said.

Olivia had seen such a change in Heath in a short time. The sullen, self-centered person who'd come through the door on the first afternoon was gone. A man with compassion and renewed faith had blossomed inside that tall, lanky body. His light was no longer hidden, it flickered with promise. It made sense that he'd want to share such positive changes with his family.

But does that have to exclude me, Lord?

Hours later Olivia wondered how was it possible for the day to fly by and drag on at the same time. She worked through her to-do list, never once having her mind clear of Heath. Where could he be and why would he run out on her—today of all days? It should be fun preparing the feast and decorating for the holiday. Instead it was a chore with little joy.

"Miss Livvy, I think we need to start check-in early today, don't you? It's already below freezin' and people are starting to show up. We can't let 'em hang around outside in this cold."

"Of course, Velma. Go ahead and take in clients as they arrive. We have plenty of hot drinks and snacks in the big room to tide us over until it's time to heat pizzas and start the movie."

"That was a good idea you had for tonight. Something easy to fix and a movie that will get folks settled early so we can keep workin' on tomorrow's dinner."

"Actually, it was Heath's idea." One of the many he'd jotted down on the legal pad in her office.

"Where is he today, anyway?" Velma asked. She looked around as if expecting him to be nearby.

Olivia hitched both shoulders, trying not to let the deep sadness in her spirit show on her face.

"You're kidding?" Velma caught on anyway.

"Nobody's seen him since last night."

"Should we call the cops?"

"He's not a missing child, Velma. We don't need to file an Amber Alert."

"Did you at least tell Detective Biddle?"

"I mentioned it and he reminded me that technically Heath is free to go back to Austin whenever he's ready."

"Did you think to check the impound lot to find out if he'd picked up his car? I sure hope he's not afoot in this cold. That old coat of his wouldn't make a good bathmat. It'd be worthless on a night like tonight."

"He's a grown man." Olivia tried to sound convincing. "He makes his own decisions and if he up and decided to leave last night that's nobody's business but his."

"But what if he—"

Velma got a *talk to the hand* gesture in her face and then Olivia tapped on the back of her wrist to indicate the time.

"It's getting late and you said yourself people need to be checked in."

Taking the hint, Velma trudged away.

"I'm just sayin'," she muttered, loud enough to be heard.

Olivia felt a lump of despair gathering in her throat. She made a beeline for her private stairwell and sprinted up the steps. Inside the apartment she leaned her backside against the door, and cupped both hands together over her breastbone. She felt the painful trembling of her heart where it shuddered deep inside her body. She gulped for air as her gaze roamed the strangely unfamiliar walls. They were suddenly white, devoid of all color and movement. Devoid of the love that touched them for a time.

Like me, like my life.

She bent at the waist to catch her breath, determined not to cry.

"Oh, Father, why would You send me love and then rip it away? Why would You let me feel this abandonment again?"

The black phone rang. She straightened, crossed to the small kitchen and lifted the receiver to her ear assuming it was Velma or Amos.

"I'll be downstairs in a minute."

"It's me."

Olivia held her breath, afraid to exhale. Fear and pressure expanded in her lungs till she thought they might burst.

Heath leaned against the cold brick wall, sheltered from the wind but still chilled to the marrow. "I'm sorry I left without so much as a note. I thought I'd be back by now."

"You're coming back?"

"Probably not."

"Heath, what's going on? Are you in some

kind of trouble?" He squeezed his eyes tight against the worry in her voice.

"Nothin' I can't handle, but I have to head home tonight." He prayed he'd be sleeping in his own bed and not on a tray in the morgue.

"Detective Biddle's been here all day. Is there something he can do to help you?"

"No, but I'd appreciate it if you'd let him know I checked in with you. And if you find anything I left behind, he'll know where to send it."

"Okay." She was a dry twig about to break. Another woman's patience would have snapped already.

Heath could just imagine righteous anger reaching the boiling point in Olivia's core. That was good. She needed to think his main concern was being off the community service hook. She needed to remember that he was a selfish creep.

A creep who loved her and might never get the chance to say so again in this life.

"Olivia, listen to me. I need to tell you something."

"Sure, whatever." She was fed up with his needs, his drama, his glass that might always be half-empty. She ought to hang up the phone, but she didn't. She waited.

"I love you." He said the words as tenderly as his chattering teeth would allow.

She was silent. What was she thinking?

"I want to thank you for everything you've taught me about myself, and about God."

"Why are you being so secretive, disappearing like this?" she demanded to know. "If you love me, then we can work this out, Heath. Living an hour apart is not a death sentence."

Depending on how things went down tonight, just living in the same state could be a death sentence. But she could never know that.

"It's not about logistics."

"Then what is it about, Heath? Please, talk to me." Her anger turned to pleading.

The team was waiting, one of the men signaling for him to join them.

"I don't have time to explain. I have to go."

"Heath—"

"I love you, Olivia."

His thumb mashed the OFF button of the secured cell and he slid it through the neck of his body armor, down into a thermal shirt pocket.

"Lord, You put me into Olivia's life for this moment, to protect her. Please let me live long enough to find out if You have other plans for us, too."

He tugged a navy wool cap close around his blackened face and gave the Glock in his shoulder holster a reassuring touch.

"Time to surprise the bad guys. Let's roll."

Chapter Twenty-Two

❧

Thanksgiving was Olivia's favorite holiday. Even after her mother's lingering death, even after her father fled like a coward, Olivia was still able to count her blessings on Thanksgiving. But today she was acutely aware that it was a season for family, something she lacked. She'd crafted one as best she could at Table of Hope, but it wasn't the same. She might never feel complete again.

Last night she'd worked beside her residents and the Biddles until her vision blurred with fatigue. The deep sleep that took over in the wee hours only lasted a brief time, and then Olivia jolted awake with a heavy feeling of dread for Heath. Her efforts to redial the phone he'd called from proved it was programmed to block the function. There was no record of Heath Stone with Austin directory assistance.

Where could he be?

The final hours of preparation Thursday morning and the service of the bountiful meal at noon were a haze in Olivia's blur of exhaustion. She was grateful that Peggy and Velma were too busy to be in her business. And the men were abuzz about a massive drug bust that had taken place in a secluded bus parking lot near the zoo in the predawn hours.

The local news reported four men arrested and two fatalities; one a young male informant and the other a Hispanic man who was in the country illegally. The media seemed caught off guard, evidently misled by their sources to anticipate the activity in another part of town.

Olivia hated that something so foreign to Table of Hope had been the main topic of conversation during their first Thanksgiving dinner.

"Did you hear about that load of pills being confiscated last night?"

"Yeah, the reporter said the cops were originally investigating drugs being sold someplace around here but it turns out they were wrong."

"Thank goodness. It's bad enough we can't count on a roof over our heads. We gotta worry about drug dealers, too?"

"The police suspect the guy who got killed was part of the *La Familia* cartel from Mexico. You remember they were behind that massive meth bust in Dallas a while back."

The speculation droned on and on until it overshadowed the meal. If Olivia had the energy, she'd rant in protest. Instead, she used the last of her steam to help move folks toward the dessert buffet so cleanup could begin in the dining area.

The big room was filled to overflowing with clients enjoying hot drinks before the television as they waited for the day's football marathon to begin. Everyone was grateful to be spending the time indoors, away from the dangerous freeze that had settled over the city.

Olivia prepared to accept an obligatory slice of pumpkin pie from Peggy, who manned the dessert tables. The woman had been a godsend, keeping the atmosphere cheerful and the day's activities on track with embarrassingly little involvement from Olivia.

"You okay, honey?" Peggy kept her voice low as she added a fat dollop of whipped cream to the pie. "Why don't you run up to your rooms and try to catch a nap while everybody's full and lazy? I'll bet every bunk in the place will have a sleeping body in it within the hour."

"I can't rest until I know where he is, Peggy. Something was wrong when he called last night. I feel it in here." Olivia pressed one hand against her chest. "Can't Bill do *something?*"

"Like what?"

"Get me a home address? I can't find any record for Heath Stone in Austin."

Peggy's gaze fell away while she silently cut slices of pie and cake, lining them up on the edge of the table. Frown lines deepened in her face as she seemed to struggle with a response.

"Peggy, you know something, don't you?"

She still didn't answer.

Olivia grasped her friend by the wrist. Their eyes met. "Please," she pleaded.

Peggy tugged her arm free and pulled off the gloves she wore for serving. "Give me a minute and I'll meet you upstairs."

The minute stretched to fifteen as Olivia paced the short distance from one side of her apartment to the other. She yanked the door wide when footsteps approached. Peggy and Detective Biddle filed inside, faces blank of expression.

"Let's sit down," he insisted. Peggy put an arm around Olivia's waist and guided her toward the small dinette. Biddle reached across the tile tabletop and rested his big hand over his wife's. They exchanged a glance and Peggy nodded. "You have to tell her, Bill."

"I'm going way outside of protocol by doing this."

"Please," Olivia begged. "I need to know what's happened to Heath."

Biddle exhaled, seemed to make up his mind.

"Heath wasn't here doing community service. He's an undercover cop who works drugs." Biddle spit out the truth.

Olivia's spine hit the back of the chair as if she'd been pushed. Hard. "What's that got to do with my shelter?"

"All our intelligence pointed to Table of Hope as a source of distribution. The Feds thought there was a chance your old man could be involved, laundering money in and out of the country. The only way to find out for sure was to put somebody inside."

"Heath."

"Yep." Biddle nodded. "He figured out pretty early that you were clean."

"He suspected *me?*" her voice rose.

"You can't blame the guy for doing his job. He put himself on the line last night and saved you a lot of heartache by drawing that bust away from here. Otherwise, the news trucks would be out front instead of over by the zoo."

"Where is he right now?"

Biddle fished a slip of paper from his pocket and slid it across the table to Olivia. She stared at what was written.

"That's his home address but with so much to do down at the station following a bust with fatalities, it's unlikely he's made it there already," Biddle explained.

"In Austin?"

"In Waco. About ten minutes from here."

When Heath dragged through the door a half hour earlier, it seemed he'd been picked up by aliens and dropped into a parallel universe. The home that had been empty and quiet since his folks moved away was bustling with activity, sound and smells. Every television in the place was turned to a different station so his father could wander from room to room and keep his eye on the college games.

In the kitchen three beautiful women and a strange-looking teenage girl were pulling together a hasty feast. Heath stood in the doorway, his hair still damp from his shower and watched their frantic activity. As amazing as it was to be suddenly surrounded by his family, Heath felt incomplete. As much as he hated to turn around and leave, he had to go to Olivia right away and explain.

"Son, are you about to starve? It's a good thing you gave us a couple days' notice because there wasn't a bite to eat in this house." His mom turned from the countertop where she was scooping up juices from the roasting pan and dumping them back over the turkey.

"That must be how he stays so thin," the young girl with the spiked hair and pierced nose commented. She raked him up and down with smudgy eyes, looking like somebody should take a washcloth to her face.

"Oh, Dana, stop worrying about your weight," his sister Erin coached her daughter. "When spring soccer starts, those few pounds you want to lose will melt off faster than your dad can bake an apple pie." Erin turned her gaze to Heath. "But I do agree our baby brother needs to be fattened up a bit."

Smiling into Erin's face was like smiling at his own reflection, the family resemblance was so strong. Heath hurt with the need to share this new sense of connection with Olivia.

"I'd be jealous of that skinny body of his if I didn't enjoy my curves so much," his older sister teased. "You and I have that in common, Dana." Alison was a vision in her colorful dress and cowboy boots with her long red hair caught in a braid that hung across her shoulder.

"Let me help you with that, Mom." He hurried across the floor to lift the turkey and slide it into the waiting oven. "Want me to mash those potatoes for you?"

She wiped her fingertips on her apron and then placed the back of her hand against his forehead.

"What are you doing?" He squinted, confused.

"I'm checking to see if you have a fever. You've never offered to help in the kitchen before, so I figured you must be sick."

He tenderly squeezed his mother's hand and joined in the laughter at his expense. "Very funny."

"Where did you ever learn to mash potatoes?" She was skeptical and rightly so.

"You'd be surprised what I've learned recently."

"Heath," his dad said as he walked from the hallway into the kitchen, "you have company." He stepped aside.

The most incredible dark eyes this side of heaven fixed Heath with an accusing stare.

"Olivia?" he breathed, unbelieving.

Her mouth popped open like words wanted out but couldn't get past her lips. She looked from one stranger to the next trying to understand the cozy scene in the room. A small cry escaped her throat as she turned around and marched out.

Shock held him frozen, but only for a moment.

"Wait!" He rushed toward the front room. She was already out the door, stomping toward the red truck parked beside his black SUV. "Will you let me explain?" His words were white puffs in the freezing air. "I was about to come get you."

She yanked open her Chevy's creaky door and vaulted into the driver's seat, sending her knit cap flying across the frozen lawn. Heath grabbed the doorframe before she could slam and lock it.

"Come back inside so we can talk."

"You mean so you can lie some more."

"Please, Olivia." He begged for a chance to explain. He'd known this time would come. "It was part of the job."

"Yeah, I know. Biddle told me all about your cover and your suspicions, how you figured out for yourself that I was in the clear. How'd you manage that, by poking around in my dresser drawers?"

"To be honest, yes."

She jammed the key in the ignition, twisted it clockwise. Nothing happened. She tried again but the truck refused to crank.

Thank you, God!

"Let's go back inside so you can meet my family. It's gosh-awful cold out here." He buffed his palms over his bare arms.

Olivia grabbed her bag and slung the strap over her shoulder as she hopped down from the seat. In three long strides she snatched up her cap, crammed it on her head and then stomped down the street. He sprinted for the front porch where his father was waiting, a warm jacket in one hand and keys in the other. He tossed them to his son.

"I'll be back as soon as I can," Heath called to his father, and then added, "Dad, I've always loved you and Mom."

"We've always known it, son."

Olivia didn't need to turn her head to know who was driving the big SUV as it pulled alongside her.

"I'll take you back to the shelter, just get in," Heath shouted through the open window.

Her toes were numb—she didn't have any choice. She nodded, he jammed on the brake and she climbed inside.

Her heart had hurt so miserably only a couple of hours before, but it seemed to have lost all sensation. Maybe even the will to beat. The anger and betrayal were so intense they eclipsed the fear that had robbed her of a night's rest. She rode in silence for as long as she could stand it. She deserved some honest answers.

"Who are those people?"

"My parents and my two sisters. The Goth kid is my niece."

"You have *sisters?*"

He nodded. "I never met them before today."

"Yeah, sure."

He had the good sense not to argue.

"Whose house is that?"

"Mine. I bought it from my folks a couple years ago so I could get them to leave town."

"You grew up right here? Never lived in Austin at all."

"That's right."

"You're a Waco cop."

"Undercover for the last seven years. That's why I never hooked up with my sisters when they tried to reach me. I couldn't risk exposing them to my work."

"But you didn't have any problem exposing me, did you, Heath?"

He turned into the service entrance beside Table of Hope and pressed on the brake.

"You were a *suspect,* Olivia. It was my job to find out if you were guilty."

"So you lied to me over and over and over."

"I lie for a living. I say whatever my cover requires to keep me alive and get the job done."

She searched in her purse, and when her fingers grazed the spiky wad she grabbed the keys. She pushed open the heavy vehicle door letting in a blast of frigid air.

"Congratulations, you're alive and you got the job done." She slid to the ground, then turned back to face him, noting the familiar SUV. "Whose vehicle is this?"

"Mine." He shook his head like he knew it was useless to explain. "I'm so sorry. If you'll just let me come inside, I'll tell you everything."

She heard the apology in his voice, saw the sadness in his eyes. Too bad.

"Happy Thanksgiving, Heath." She closed the door and walked away.

Inside the back entrance the hallway was blessedly warm and empty. Conversation and cheers echoed from the big room. Olivia let herself into her apartment, folded into a heap on her bed and stared at the dresser that Heath had searched.

She muffled her cries with the stocking cap that was all she had left of her daddy and sobbed as her hardened heart began to thaw. The pain was jagged and cold like the shattering of icicles as they fell from the eaves of Table of Hope.

Chapter Twenty-Three

Saturday morning Olivia splashed her eyes with icy cold water and prayed that the puffiness would be less noticeable by the afternoon. Twenty-four hours of blubbering and wrestling with the Holy Spirit had left her worn out but convinced that God would somehow use this pain for her good and His glory.

"Miss Livvy, can I come in?" Amos called from the stairwell as he rapped his knuckles on the apartment door.

"Of course," she answered, turning the bolt allowing him to enter.

They embraced for a moment, awkward as they hadn't yet spoken since her discovery of Heath's deception.

"Thanks for taking care of everything so I could have a couple of days to myself. I don't know what I'd do without you." She settled into her favorite rocker and motioned for Amos to take the sofa. He sat at the far end.

"Well, here's the thing." His voice wavered. "My daughter asked me to come to Houston and live with her for a spell. She has a little guest-room and I could have my own space."

Olivia held her breath and waited for the rest, not sure her heart could take another loss so quickly.

"That sounds perfect." She looked toward the frosted window to hide the hot tears she thought had drained dry.

Amos scooted down the sofa until he was close enough to take her hand.

"Yeah, I know it *sounds* perfect, but before long we'd both be sorry we were stuck under the same roof. So I told her a visit would be nice, but I plan to keep livin' in Waco. Miss Livvy, I'd like to stay here and work with you for as long as you'll have me."

Olivia leaned forward, wrapped her arms around Amos's scrawny body and hugged him fiercely. "I'll do a lot better than that. We'll figure out how to give you some private living space and I'll hire you to help me manage the shelter. I need you, Amos. I can't do this all by myself and paint, too."

"So, you really want to do the art thing, huh?"

"I do." She allowed herself a relieved smile over the decision. "It's a gift God's given me and I owe it to Him to see how far I can take it. So would you stay with me and be my partner, Amos?"

"First I need to tell you something."

"Anything."

"I knew about Heath, being undercover and all. I even worked with him and Biddle right at the end. You see, the night Nick needed to talk to somebody, it was to confess that he'd been involved with trafficking some of those sorry pills. He's just a stupid kid, doing it to make some fast money, thinkin' that was a way to get back on his feet. Heath was able to get Nick off with a year of probation for cooperating and telling us where the big drop was being made. That's what set the whole plan in motion and got our town rid of those spineless drug dealers."

"Where's Nick now?"

"Downstairs, scrubbin' my kitchen floor with a toothbrush." Amos grinned. "Biddle decided to turn the community service idea into the real thing. If you'll allow it, Nick will be with us until his probation is up. I'll work him like a rented mule."

"That's fine with me," she agreed. "Everybody deserves a second chance."

"Later today I want you to remember that,"

Amos said softly. "We all wish we could change things in our past but God doesn't give us a Mulligan in this life. Instead He commanded us to forgive and love one another and that's the best do-over of all."

Heath stepped inside the Studio Gallery and paused to catch his breath. His pulse was racing and he could feel the throbbing in his temples. The place was packed.

Thank you, Lord! For everything Olivia's done for the community, she is so deserving of this opportunity.

He straightened the tie his dad had loaned him and checked the button on his suit jacket to make sure it was still tight where his niece had sewn it on *with red thread*. He felt in the pocket of his dress slacks for the wad of tissue his mom had given him. Lastly, he looked down at the shiny new pair of cowboy boots his sisters had brought him from West Texas, insisting they wanted their baby brother to have a memorable gift from their reunion. If the pointy toes kept hurting his feet, they'd be memorable all right.

Satisfied that he was presentable, Heath stretched tall and studied the room until he spotted Olivia's profile. Her thick black hair perfectly framing her face, her head held high, her unadorned eyes crinkled by some interest, her lips curved by her always positive temperament. She laughed, turned to someone at her side, glanced up for a moment and spotted him. Her eyes opened wider, as if her vision couldn't be trusted. He prayed the surprise in her face was a good thing. He prayed it would still be there by the time he squeezed through the bodies that separated them. He prayed it wasn't too late.

She met him more than halfway, bringing him a flute of something pink with bubbles floating to the top.

"What's this?" He took the tall skinny glass and held it suspiciously to the light.

"Truth serum," she deadpanned.

"In that case—" He touched his crystal rim to hers. "Cheers." The entire glass of fruity pink seltzer went down well, leaving a fizzy feeling in his mouth.

"Want seconds?"

"That's not necessary. Believe me."

"How can I ever believe you again, Heath?"

"You have to give me another chance. I promise I'll earn your trust, Olivia."

"I don't even know who you are."

"Yes, you do. There was more truth than lies, but I was afraid to tell you everything." He gave their glasses to a passing waiter, took her soft hand in his and guided her to a quiet corner of the gallery where a nook of her paintings offered them privacy.

"My amazing and kind Olivia." Heath touched her cheek tenderly hoping she wouldn't reject him. "My parents didn't die together in an accident like I said. The truth is my two sisters and I come from a very violent home. Our father killed our mother and went to prison, where he died a few years ago. The three of us were split up in the foster care system. I was adopted, Alison and Erin weren't.

"Ever since I discovered my history, I've been afraid it was also my legacy. I expected that I'd be lacking, so I never looked for fullness in life. But you helped me remember that God is a God of second chances. The department, my parents, and my sisters have all given me the opportunity to be a new man. But no human other than you can make me complete."

He fished for the tissue in his pocket and dropped to one knee.

"Oh, no!" Olivia's hands flew to cover her mouth.

"No?" Heath prepared to stand.

"No, I mean yes!" She pressed her palms to his shoulders pushing him back to his knee. "You just stunned and surprised me."

"I'd like to surprise you for the rest of our lives, if you'll let me. I love you, Olivia."

"Wait." Olivia pulled him to his feet and tugged him to the same bench where they sat on their first visit. "How will we do this? You know Table of Hope isn't just my mission. It's my life."

"Work can't be your life any more than it can be mine. I'm moving to Biddle's division so I can focus on computer crime. Then you won't have to worry about me being on the street. If you'll delegate some stuff to Amos, you can take a couple of days off each week to paint. I'm sure there must be a great guy beneath the surface of that miserable old curmudgeon, so if you want we could hire him, give him your apartment."

"If Amos had my place, where does that leave me?"

Heath smiled, unsure if he'd led her to this moment or she'd led him. Either way, he was right where he wanted to be. He got back on one knee and took her hand, offered her the twinkling diamond her mother had passed on from his grandmother.

"In *our* home. Together we'll become part of my family, whoever and wherever they are. That is if you still love me, Olivia. Please let me hear it from your lips again."

"I love you, my darlin'." Her eyes were bright with emotion, nothing held back. "I had to say it at least once that night in the doughnut shop and now God's made a way for me to say it to you forever."

Heath reached for her hand to slip on the ring. It fit. Just as her world would fit his.

Perfectly.

Heath's life with Olivia was a cup of new possibility, full and overflowing.

* * * * *

Dear Reader,

I trust you enjoyed Heath and Olivia's Thanksgiving story. This unique holiday is not about giving gifts, but about giving thanks for the people God has used to bless our lives in ways we may never realize this side of eternity. The Thanksgiving meal truly is a table of hope.

This book wraps up my series on a brother and two sisters separated as children by family violence. Our culture might say they were collateral damage, casualties of a modern society. But through their faith Alison, Erin and Heath each overcame the world's obstacles to become the people God intended them to be.

During this season of thanksgiving may you be grateful for those in your life who live in the belief that all things are possible with Jesus Christ.

Until we meet again, let your light shine!

Mae Nunn

QUESTIONS FOR DISCUSSION

1. On any given night in America between 70,000 and two million people are homeless. Have you ever volunteered at a homeless shelter or soup kitchen? Why or why not?

2. Families constitute about one third of the homeless population and are the fastest growing group of homeless people. How can your book club or community group work together to help a homeless family?

3. Olivia's faith and Christian worldview impacted everything in her life. Are you able to look at the world through the lens of your relationship with Christ?

4. Heath was raised in a loving adoptive home but never felt fully connected with his parents. Do you believe there's a hardwired need for a person to know their birth parents in order to feel complete?

5. Heath went into the foster care system as a small child and was lucky to be adopted. How much do you know about foster care in your city or state? Would you consider being a foster parent?

6. Even though she'd suffered loss and abandonment at a young age, Olivia was still very trusting of basic human nature. Could you be as trusting and forgiving? Why or why not?

7. Heath worked for so long as an undercover cop that he began to lose himself in his "characters" and wasn't sure he liked his personality any longer. What could he have done to stay more in touch with his true self?

8. We all know someone with a glass-half-empty way of looking at life. What tactics could you use to encourage such a person to see the world from a more positive perspective? To count their blessings?

9. Amos was starting his life over at an age when he should have been enjoying his senior years. Can you relate to being in that situation? Do you know someone dealing with such a circumstance?

10. Nick thought he'd make a quick buck to jump-start his income. I know someone who paid for that kind of thinking by spending eighteen months of his life in prison. What makes a person risk their long-term freedom for the short-term payout?

11. Though Heath and Olivia had very different ways of looking at the world, it didn't keep them from falling in love. Why do you think opposites attract?

12. The Christian teaching of Heath's childhood came back to him in a practical way in his adulthood. Do you recall a time when Biblical principles you never understood as a child made sense to you as a grown up?

13. Heath was grateful to have a second chance for a relationship with his sisters. But even the best of sibling relationships can be trying at times. Can you think of a situation when a sister or brother almost made you lose your religion?

14. There are some extremely difficult family relationships that seem impossible to overcome. But nothing is impossible with our God. Was there ever a time when you sought spiritual guidance in order to resolve a dispute within your family?

15. Are you new to Love Inspired books or have you been reading them for years? Are you aware we now have historical and suspense as well as contemporary novels? Please visit www.LoveInspiredAuthors.com. We'd love to hear from you!

LARGER PRINT BOOKS!

GET 2 FREE LARGER PRINT NOVELS PLUS 2 FREE MYSTERY GIFTS

Love Inspired®

Larger print novels are now available...

YES! Please send me 2 FREE LARGER PRINT Love Inspired® novels and my 2 FREE mystery gifts (gifts are valued at $10). After receiving them, if I don't wish to receive any more books, I can return the shipping statement marked "cancel." If I don't cancel, I will receive 3 brand-new novels every month and be billed just $4.74 per book, a savings of $1.51 off the cover price, plus 25¢ shipping and handling per book and applicable taxes, if any*. I understand that accepting the 2 free books and gifts places me under no obligation to buy anything. I can always return a shipment and cancel at any time. Even if I never buy another book from Steeple Hill, the two free books and gifts are mine to keep forever.

101 IAN EYP2

Name (PLEASE PRINT)

Address   Apt. #

City   State   Zip

Signature (if under 18, a parent or guardian must sign)

Mail to Steeple Hill Reader Service:

P.O. BOX 1867 Buffalo, NY 14240-1867

Are you a current Love Inspired subscriber and want to receive the larger print edition?
Call 1-800-873-8635 today!

* Terms and prices subject to change without notice. Prices do not include applicable taxes. Sales tax applicable in N.Y. This offer is limited to one order per household. All orders subject to approval. Credit or debit balances in a customer's account(s) may be offset by any other outstanding balance owed by or to the customer. Please allow 4 to 6 weeks for delivery. Offer available while quantities last.

Your Privacy: Steeple Hill Books is committed to protecting your privacy. Our Privacy Policy is available online at www.SteepleHill.com or upon request from the Reader Service. From time to time we make our lists of customers available to reputable third parties who may have a product or service of interest to you. If you would prefer we not share your name and address, please check here. ☐

BIABLPS09PI

LARGER-PRINT BOOKS!

**GET 2 FREE
LARGER-PRINT NOVELS
PLUS 2 FREE
MYSTERY GIFTS**

Love Inspired®

SUSPENSE
RIVETING INSPIRATIONAL ROMANCE

Larger-print novels are now available...

Love Inspired.
SUSPENSE

RIVETING INSPIRATIONAL ROMANCE

Watch for our new series of
edge-of-your-seat suspense novels.
These contemporary tales
of intrigue and romance
feature Christian characters
facing challenges to their faith...
and their lives!

NOW AVAILABLE IN REGULAR
& LARGER-PRINT FORMATS

Steeple
Hill®

Visit:
www.SteepleHill.com